FIRE AND HONEY

FIRE AND HONEY

C.J. EVANS

The Book Guild Ltd

First published in Great Britain in 2017 by
The Book Guild Ltd
9 Priory Business Park
Wistow Road, Kibworth
Leicestershire, LE8 0RX
Freephone: 0800 999 2982
www.bookguild.co.uk
Email: info@bookguild.co.uk
Twitter: @bookguild

Typeset in Minion Pro

Printed and bound in the UK by TJ International, Padstow, Cornwall

ISBN 978 1912083 824

British Library Cataloguing in Publication Data.
A catalogue record for this book is available from the British Library.

A big thank you to my wonderful wife and best friend for all her help and hard work. Also to my lovely daughter Catrina for the same, and love to my son Martin for his enthusiasm. My sister Lorraine for her encouragement and support, and last, but not least, my marvelous sister-in-law Chris for her invaluable critique.

1

SUSAN

Most of the trees in Arcadia Avenue had long since withered and given up their tenuous grip on life, victims of Dutch elm disease and the herbicidal cocktail of modern-day pollutants. Consequently the rapture of symphonic bird song that would rise in volume as the sun rose higher in the pale blue sky had diminished to the point of extinction.

This sleepy, once leafy, suburb of London is where at, number one Arcadia Avenue, I, Susan Payne was born and subsequently brought up. Its red brick façade standing out amongst the neighbouring dwellings with their dark dank dingy rendered walls, being under constant attack from the green, slimy mould that surreptitiously crept from the ground upwards. The bright white glossed windows shone with a brilliant lustre, the glass sparkled and shimmered, not a solitary finger mark or any other abrasion was allowed to tarnish the illusion of grandeur. Even our feathered friends avoided soiling this house. The small, but neat front garden, with its rows of marigolds, planted with military precision, stood out among the rough, untidy, overgrown gardens that festooned the area.

When you walked through the glossy varnished hardwood front door, the smell of furniture polish and potpourri sank menacingly into your lungs. Under the hall rug, the parquet flooring shimmered with a deep shine and walking on the rug required some dexterity, akin to the first time on an ice rink. Inside the rooms were tastefully decorated and every piece of furniture kept formerly in its place. The deep impression in the thick sumptuous carpet pile left by the castors, a testament that moving anything from its place would incur the unadulterated wrath of Mother. Books stood like soldiers standing to attention on the shelves and were arranged in chronological order; there was little danger of putting them back in the wrong place as the only time they were disturbed was when Mother dusted the shelves.

Out through the kitchen, where the smell of freshly baked bread and the ever constant smell of coffee percolating engulfed the senses, was the door to the back garden. Here is where I spent most of my adolescent years. I have nothing but fond memories of those long hot sultry halcyon days of summer spent in the secluded garden, awash with its own character, more matured than mulled wine. A taste not to everyone's palate perhaps, but unique nonetheless. I recalled a midsummer's morning watching a Red Admiral butterfly perched majestically upon a golden gooseberry bush, its red opulent wings as though dusted with a lady's blusher, almost daring me to touch it, but I knew if I did it may never fly again.

For so long ours had been the quintessential English garden. The rose trees in circular beds dug into the lawn. The geraniums and Father's prize dahlias taking pride of place. The six-foot-high sunflower stood next to the rotting shed with its head hung, as if in shame, every time the sun dispersed behind a cloud. Shrubs grew in abundant clusters, intertwined with tall coarse grass that invaded their space, threatening to depose their natural right to reign supreme, with its feverish growth. In one corner, at the furthest reaches of the garden, lay the pond surrounded by an army of thistles and uninhabited weed growth that was Nirvana for the myriad of small creatures that dwelt there under every rock and stone. Hovering inches from a water lily on the algae green pond and perilously close to a loitering Golden Carp was that king of kings the majestic dragonfly, upon its head a purple crown, its wings a pastiche of infinite colour. Its fleeting life expired by tomorrow's dawn.

Sadly my mother and father died while I was still in my late teens: Mother from a sudden illness that robbed her of her twilight years and, being unable to cope without the woman who governed his every thought and daily routine, my father committed suicide. He was so bereft of his wife's sudden parting that he couldn't go on without her even though, when she was alive, he'd often hide in the shed to be beyond her watchful gaze. His love for me wasn't diminished by his decision to end his life, his mind being unbalanced and blinded by grief. I had to suffer the heartbreak of losing my mum and had to grieve alone after my dad ended his life, which made me quite resentful at first. How could my dad do that to me when I needed him to be there to help me grief for my mum: It wasn't till later that I understood how destructive grief could be and how utterly distraught my father must have been to leave the daughter, that he idolised so much, behind. The house that was once more of a shrine than a home had been sold, leaving me with a welcomed inheritance of moderate proportions. I live alone these days in a small but functional flat, a ten minute walk from the factory where I work as a clerk. My inheritance would give me the chance to fulfil one of my ambitions: to go on holiday to the Caribbean Isles. I had heard so many stories about the Caribbean from my uncle, whom I sometimes stayed with during the long summer holidays. He lived in a wonderful house with an enormous garden that was full of apple trees, which hung with red ripe apples ready to be plundered. Amongst the orchard were his bee hives, he loved the taste of fresh honey. At the bottom of the garden a silky green river gently meandered by.

The house was situated in a small hamlet just outside of Oxford. I often visited Oxford whilst I was there. The grandeur of the places of learning – the tall dreamy spires and ancient cobbled streets – overwhelmed me with their elegance. Even as a schoolgirl I had indulged my erotic fantasies, my vivacious appetite for sex soon entered a more sinister dawn when, at just sixteen, I flirted with my Uncle Eric, knowing his wife, several years his junior, had long since left him to fend for himself. In truth he did not take much cajoling from me as he had always had a penchant for young girls. Perhaps it was their innocence that attracted him or their tight virginal bodies, although

4

this did not apply in my case, I had lost my virginity in the bike shed with Sam Goodall before my 15th birthday. What started out as a bit of a fumble went too far and I experienced my first orgasm. In truth, it was all a bit frenzied and rushed, and not really that edifying. I have since learnt how to use my not inconsiderable feminine charm to manipulate the male fraternity into doing whatever I wanted. I seemed able to make men simply melt with my alluring provocative glance and seductive smile.

Late one sunny July afternoon, after enjoying a pleasant cream tea on the lawn, Eric and I settled down together under the shade of a willow tree; we were soon completely naked and fondling each other feverishly. Suddenly Eric got up and wandered over to the bee hives; he took out a comb of honey, as the bees swarmed around his head and naked body. He acted on impulse and did not take his usual precautions against being stung; however, he had great confidence in his bees and seldom got stung, even when on this occasion he had been foolhardy. "It's just as well they didn't sting you on your marvellous manhood, my sweet," I giggled, "or I would have had to make it better for you." I grinned seductively.

I laid outstretched on the grass, my legs spread wide, and wondered what Eric was intending to do. Eric stood teasingly over me straddling my young, tantalising, wanton body. He began to pour the freshly made honey over my voluptuous pink breasts and down the full length of my body. It laid in a sticky golden pool at the pit of my stomach and trickled down between my legs. Eric sank to his knees and seductively began to lick the honey from my heaving breasts, my back arched in pleasure and with my body sizzling as his tongue travelled the length of my body, exploring every insatiable inch of flesh. My moans of ecstasy became uncontrollable screams of exultant joy as Eric entered my pot of honey. It was like extracting nectar from a wild flower and he felt like a giant bee tasting one of nature's most exotic treasures.

Once Eric had finished feasting on my honey-soaked, naked body, he climbed on top of me, his hairy chest sticking to my fulsome breasts. As the hours passed the sun's last rays disappeared below the horizon as the faint glow of the moon took its place, Eric took me to the stars and beyond. I gazed skyward, my head buzzing with excitement, as under the jewelled moon love's golden copulations flowed whilst soft words of love from honeyed lips fell upon my ears. A feeling of deep satisfaction consumed my body in a swathe of gentle warmth as Uncle Eric spewed his seeds over my honey-soaked pubic hair.

After the erotic sexual encounter with Uncle Eric there were many more subsequent similar assignations, but in time, I got a little tired of his over romantic escapades and desired the company of someone near my own age. The next time I went to stay with Uncle Eric he took me into the quaint small local village where he would go to watch the cricket team play on the green in the centre of the village. As an ex-player himself he knew a lot of the players and their wives. His banter with some of the younger prettier ladies suggested that they were more than casual acquaintances; I could tell by the lecherous way his eyes scanned their curvaceous bodies and the furtive glances at any possible available young filly. He was now an honorary member of the club and enjoyed certain privileges. He gave up playing long ago but still maintained an interest in the club's fortunes. He had access to the cricket pavilion and was invited to afternoon tea with the players and the committee. A sumptuous tea was always provided by the dutiful wives of the players and they were justifiably proud of their efforts.

On one midsummer's barmy Sunday afternoon I was sat with my Uncle Eric on the village green awaiting the arrival, to the crease, of the opposition's opening batsman. I was expressly interested in watching our handsome fast bowler, Christian Bail. An incredibly apt name for a bowler, I mused. All the men enthused over his action and swing etc., but my interest was more primeval. I was entranced by the seductive way he rubbed that shiny leather ball up and down his groin. As he made his run up he gave a furtive glance in my direction. He released the ball like a sling shot aimed squarely at the centre of the wicket. I could not help noticing the girth of Christian's middle wicket and salivated at the thought of being impaled upon his middle stump. He certainly bowls this maiden over! There was something quite sensual about the sound of leather against willow, almost like the crack of a whip upon a bare cheek and almost as pleasurable. It wasn't long before the poor hapless batsman succumbed to a wickedly fast delivery that removed the bails, leaving the batsman with a long meandering walk to the pavilion.

Christian was now rested and a spin bowler was

introduced, leaving him to take up a fielding position close to where I was sitting. I crossed my legs in my short white skirt revealing a chunk of thigh and a glimpse of my knickers, hoping to attract his attention; of course I didn't want to disturb his concentration. My uncle noticed my flirtatious gesture and put his hand on my knees then slid it up all the way to my thigh. He looked at me and smiled his customary sensual grins evoking thoughts of past assignations. I emphatically pushed his hand away leaving him in no doubt that on this occasion I was not interested in his advances. NO, it was Christian's hand that I wanted to feel sliding up the inside of my leg. Just the thought of his hand between my legs made me tingle and gave me goosebumps. Just at that moment Christian was called into action as the batsman skied a wayward delivery. Christian leapt athletically into the air, catching the ball with one hand.

I clapped and cheered rather too enthusiastically for the sober conservative crowd, which drew some attention and some disparaging remarks aimed in my direction. I responded with a two-fingered gesture which attracted a hail of tut tuts from the village idiots. More importantly and pertinent was the fact that Christian was staring straight at me, his penetrating crystal blue eyes making me weak at the knees. I shifted nervously on my seat, being sure to show off even more of my womanly charms. I did my Sharon Stone, impression letting him see what was on offer. You didn't need a degree in Quantum Physics to feel the chemistry that existed between us. An attraction like the gravitational pull of the moon upon the oceans and as impossible to resist. I leapt to

8

my feet and flung my arms around his neck, I kissed him passionately on the lips and whispered in his ear, "Meet me behind the pavilion later." I coyly resumed my poise and returned to my seat. Christian was shocked and not a little embarrassed by my outpouring of passion, but still managed to give me a wink and a cheeky grin as he nodded in reply, suggesting he was up for a meet later. The cricket match seemed to last forever, but the village team eventually won convincingly.

After the tea and sandwiches and some boring small talk I managed to escape my uncle's clawing clutches to meet Christian behind the cricket pavilion. I waited for a while and was about to give up when he appeared around the corner of the pavilion. "Hello, Christian, I didn't think you were going to come," I said, fluttering my eyes.

"Oh how could I resist," he remarked playfully, "after the come on you gave me".

"Come on, me" I said coyly."I'm far too innocent for that, you must have misunderstood me," I giggled.

"I don't think so," he replied as he took me in his manly arms. As we kissed it was like the fusion of atomic particles that would erupt into a nuclear explosion of passion. A surge of electricity was pulsating through my veins as I felt his tongue in my mouth. By now it was getting dark; the sun was disappearing, to be replaced in the clear night sky by the faint glow of the moon.

Everyone had gone home, including my uncle, who was not altogether pleased by my absence, although I had assured him I would be fine and would see him later. After all I was a big girl now! The cricket green in the centre of the village was eerily quiet now. I dragged

Christian onto the pitch and straddled his middle wicket. He groaned with pleasure as he entered my crease, his seed spewing over the hard, barren batting surface. We laid undisturbed under the watchful eye of the full crimson moon for what seemed like an eternity, before disentangling ourselves and vowing to meet up again as soon as it was practical. I was determined to make the most of my transitory life, and so it was that we did indeed meet again. We did it everywhere that summer, and in the most unlikely places, which made it exciting and fun.

We did it in the pub cellar and the cricket green again. The church, Christ those pews are hard. In the pavilion changing rooms – god the smell of that male testosterone filled the air and really turned me on. One day I thought it would be a giggle if we could manage to do it in the confessional of the village Catholic church, but, God, the embarrassment when the priest slid back the door covering the grill and asking me had I any sins to declare. I screamed and said a few Hail Mary's and some unsavoury words, and ran out through the vestry, my knickers in hand and my skirt still hitched up around my waist, leaving poor Christian to explain himself to the perplexed priest. It seems I'd crossed the boundaries of what was acceptable in a sleepy narrow-minded English village. That sadly was the end of my liaison with Christian; not that I was heartbroken, it was after all pure lust. I was never in love with him but, all the same, I did miss the excitement and I wondered where my life might take me next.

Uncle Eric had regular assignations with a young

eighteen-year-old girl from the village called Andrea Stevens. I had met her on a couple of occasions whilst visiting my uncle outside the school holidays. When I and Andrea had both finished our education and embarked on our respective careers, we decided to meet up occasionally so we could swap sordid stories about Uncle Eric and generally have a giggle, as young women are want to do. We discovered, as our friendship matured, that we had quite a lot in common, apart from the lecherous Uncle Eric of course, and that we shared an ambition to travel to exotic foreign parts, such as the sun-drenched Caribbean Isles that always conjured up romantic overtones in our impressionable young minds.

It was no secret among my friends that my big ambition was to go on a long holiday to the Caribbean Isles; I longed to live out my childhood fantasies. I dreamt of meeting Mr Right somewhere on a sun-drenched island paradise, silver sand between my toes and shimmering blue waters lapping the shore. The sound of the waves crashing upon the breakers and the clink of ice in the tall slender glass of rum punch that I put to my pink lips and sip regally. Very soon my dreams would come true as the years of planning and dreaming came to fruition.

It was a lucky day when fate contrived to bring myself and Andrea together. We had totally different backgrounds and were chalk and cheese personality wise, but we got on like we had been friends all our lives. Andrea was much quieter than me and was happy staying in the background, although she was very pretty in an understated way and attracted sufficient interest from

11

the male fraternity to sometimes put me in the shade, which I positively hated. Andrea was born and brought up in Hartlepool where they are said to have once hung a monkey for being a spy. She had pretty much but not quite lost her accent through years of living down South. Andrea talked to me at length about her past, pouring out her heart and laying bare her fragility before me.

She never forgot the rows upon rows of dingy dark houses, the back alleys where she played as a child festooned with washing lines which brought the only smell of freshness to her senses. She remembered the smell of fish and chip suppers, but above all else the grey landscape that insidiously crept into her psyche and led to despair and depression. Andrea's parents had a turbulent relationship. Her father was continually in and out of work as there were not many jobs about, and his drinking made it difficult for him to hold down a job for long; consequently, he would come home from the working man's club drunk, demanding his dinner or his conjugal rights in no particular order. Worse still he abused Andrea physically, sexually and psychologically. Andrea was an only child, so she had no brothers or sisters to confide in or to seek solace. By the time she reached adolescence she was desperate to get away. The day she left Hartlepool for the last time she looked back at the dark grey totality and the just as dark and depressive memories of the past and shut the door on it forever.

2

Andrea and I climbed the steps of the gleaming silver jumbo jet as it stood on the wet Heathrow tarmac waiting to take off for the magical Caribbean sun. We anticipated hot sultry sun-filled days and dreamt of warm sensuous nights of passion. We made our way to our allocated seats and strapped ourselves in, chatting nervously to other passengers as the stewardess ran through the emergency evacuation procedure. Everyone looked cool and relaxed and dressed in the latest fashionable designer leisure wear.

I remembered to pack my Gucci shoes and genuine alligator handbag for those special nights of exotic moonlit dinner dates that I was sure I would encounter. I am supremely confident in my seductive abilities and was sure I would be able to conjure up a night of pure magic and furtive pleasure with the man of my dreams. I adorned myself with sparkling-costume jewellery that looked more expensive than it was, and bathed my soft white skin in a heavy heady scent that made a statement. Although I've never claimed to be especially sophisticated or refined, I always make the most of my looks and I arrange my hair and make-up fastidiously. When I'm out on the town some of my friends accuse me of dressing like a slut at times, but I've always subscribed to the old adage 'if you've got it flaunt it'. When it comes to men I like to think of myself as a sizzling temptress, who, like the black widow spider, would, metaphorically speaking, devour her mate. I see my tantalising powers of seduction as a testament of feminist conquest over male dominance.

I find the male sexual organ a constant source of pleasure and to that end, I made a point of packing my favourite brand of condoms so as to be sure of complete and utter safety. The last thing I wanted from a holiday romance was an unwanted pregnancy, or, perhaps, worse, some sexually transmitted disease. Men were captivated by my voluptuous figure, long brown hair, my petite face that glowed with a satin lustre, like the face of a china doll, my pretty pert lips glistening with lip gloss, almost begged to be kissed. Guys would look dreamingly into my huge green eyes and feel themselves free-falling through space, the exhilarating sensation of falling hopelessly out of control sucked the breath from their lungs and absorbed their souls.

I am about five foot ten inches tall have long slender legs and tights firm buttocks. I wriggle my sexy frame provocatively whenever I sense that I have a male audience. I have a penchant for short, tight, revealing skirts that complement my figure; I pour herself into the tightest jeans possible, and wear low-cut tops and snug fitting bras that barely managed to keep my fulsome bosom from escaping their confinement.

I had already spotted a couple of likely lads, two rows in front. I bent forward to get a better view and inadvertently allowed one of my breasts to escape their enforced confinement, momentarily raising the temperature of every red-blooded male in eye shot. However, I slowly, without undue panic, restored the offending breast back into its holster. I turned to Andrea and said in not a very quiet whisper, "God, can you see that guy; he's hung like a stallion. I wouldn't mind being his mare." At this point I mused to myself how exhilarating it would be to be a member of the mile high club. As I sat back in my seat, daydreaming images of every phallic symbol known to man running through my mind, filling my subconscious with lustful thoughts. Andrea just looked on sheepishly, almost embarrassed, by my forthright outpourings of lust and shrugged her shoulders dismissively. I am and have always been a gregarious outgoing person who likes sex; I am not ashamed of the fact and I don't see why I should be. I always think it is grossly unfair that promiscuous woman are labelled sluts when equally promiscuous men are called nice words like stud or lotharios etc. I think Andrea finds my outgoing behaviour an embarrassment but she'd better get used to it quickly as I'm not about to change anytime soon. It's who I am and cannot be little miss prim and proper and don't want to. I have become a pariah amongst my married friends, they treat me like I'm a femme fatal frightened that I'd run off with their nearest and dearest, indeed, I have become persona-non-grata in some circles. In truth I'm not interested in their boring husbands or their boring lives. I could have anyone of them with a click of my fingers but what would be the fun of that. Finding sex was easy enough, finding love was my personal holy grail, and it was proving much more elusive.

We held hands as the plane started to taxi along the rain lashed runway, the air was full of the smell of aviation fuel as the thrust from the seven four seven's powerful engines lifted us clear of the runway. We closed our eyes and dreamt of what was to come. As I relaxed after the long drive to the airport I fell into a slumber. As I slept I imagined laying on a silver tropical Barbados beach with my latest love deeply embodied in my womanhood. I wanted to feel him, to taste him, to touch the afterglow of his aura. To me, at this moment, he was the very element of life itself; like oxygen I drew breath from him, I drank from his soul the substance to sustain eternal life, like a bee drawing nectar from a wild flower. The convulsions from our copulating bodies strewn to eternal damnation among the elements beyond the constellation to be cast into oblivion through the eons of time to a portal in space to become as they began, a speck of dust or indeed a grain of sand on which I now dreamed I was laying.

The wheels of the seven-four-seven squeaked as we touched down on the smouldering tarmac, waking us with a start. As the doors of the plane were flung open an intense wall of hot air engulfed us. The heat was overpowering and took our breath away. As we disembarked from the plane we peered skyward through our Ray-Bans into the bluest sky either of us had ever seen. Scattered rays of sun, like golden spun silk threads of yarn, revealed the sea of blue above with its brilliance. The only departure from the overwhelming blue expanse above was the white fluffy cotton wool clouds that punctuated the blueness.

Myself and Andrea strolled through the airport lounge and waved our passports as I flashed my customary provocative smile. We waited at the carousel for our suitcases to arrive and were soon boarding our transfer transport to the Hotel Contessa. After about a forty-minute drive along dusty, potholed, twisting roads we came to a beautiful low-rise hotel complex with the archetypical straw thatched roof, the plastered outer walls gleaming white. Inside the entrance lobby more white walls and a cold marble floor that encouraged the feeling of a cool relaxed atmosphere, in no small measure, aided by the numerous huge fans that swirled above our heads making a whirling sound that buzzed in our ears. After Andrea and I had checked in we made our way to our rooms to unpack and unwind. The room was adequately proportioned, although it was sparsely furnished, we had all we needed and the view from the window was sublime. Stretched before our eyes was a fine white sandy beach punctuated, periodically, by gently swaying palm trees. The deep blue opulent warm Caribbean waters, that gently lapped the sandy shore, intensely drew our attention.

We decided to have a shower to cool down and to reapply our makeup before contemplating our next move. Andrea and I made our way to one of the three outside pools and sank into a poolside bar stool and ordered a long cool punch and introduced ourselves to the tall dark handsome barman; making full use of my gleaming iridescent green eyes. "So, Carlos, where is all the action around here? Where are all the eligible handsome young men hiding?" I had decided he looked like a Carlos and from there on in that is how I would refer to him.

"I'm sure you'll encounter plenty of handsome young men, miss," Carlos replied. "I can imagine a queue forming this very moment," he said as he peered down my low-cut top that was already beginning to adhere to my braless breasts as the clammy heat caused perspiration to trickle between my heaving bosom. Andrea, as usual, sat pensive, just staring straight ahead through her cool sequined eyes, sipping her ice-cold cocktail and listening to my chat-up lines with disdain.

Deep down I think Andrea would like to be more like me but she lacks the confidence and self-belief that I have in copious amounts. I don't honestly think she believes she's capable of reaching the lusty heights of sexual gratification that comes so easily to me. I'm sure, in time, I'll be able to coax out of her the animal lust that lays undiscovered in her subconscious. I'm sure she had been damaged by things that had happened to her in her past. As I continued chatting to the barman two European-looking men, in their mid-thirties, sauntered up to the bar. They were casually dressed in t-shirt and shorts, heavily tanned and quite gorgeous-looking. Andrea was first to notice them, her eyes darting about nervously and excitedly. She spun round on her stool and came face to face with a golden tanned hunk. He had the facial bone structure and firm muscular body of an Adonis. His friend too looked handsome and debonair. "Hello there," I said, my big green eyes almost bulging out of their sockets. "I'm Susan and this is my friend Andrea." I offered my hand in friendship and Miguel duly obliged and shook my hand heartily, exclaiming

"Hi I'm Miguel and this is my old friend Roman". I leant across and shook Roman's hand. Andrea leaned over me to shake Miguel and Roman's hands, introducing herself with a gleam in her sultry blue eyes.

Miguel ordered two cold beers. "Could I buy you ladies a drink?" Miguel asked in a heavy Spanish accent. I replied for myself and Andrea. "Yes please, we will have the same again, barman." "You're on holiday, yes?" said Miguel in his pigeon English.

"Yes it is our first day; we only arrived this morning." Andrea nodded in agreement and Roman glanced at her and smiled, his gleaming white teeth standing out against his tanned complexion.

"Are you on holiday?" enquired Andrea, directing her question to Roman.

"Not exactly," replied Roman in a typical Italian accent. "We're on what you might call a working holiday."

"Okay so what do you do then, Roman, is it something exciting," enquired Andrea.

"I could tell you but I would have to kill you," Roman laughed. "No, to be honest it's quite boring really, we just run our own import export business. We have a modest yacht and we carry and deliver goods between the islands most of the time."

Miguel stared at Roman with a menacing look in his eye. "I'm sure the ladies do not want to know about our dreary work, let's talk of something else," he said firmly closing the door on the subject.

After an hour or so of chatting and getting to know each other Miguel offered to take us on a tour of the island, starting with the local village. To really get a flavour of life in the Caribbean you have to mingle with the locals, smell and taste the fruits and spices of the market place. You have to see the colours and feel the human warmth of the inhabitants, the joyous smiles and the good humour that abounds. The sounds of the steel bands, reggae and ska emanating from every corner of the island bombard the senses. We left the hotel complex after changing into some more appropriate clothes for sightseeing, before meeting up with Miguel with Roman and after a short ride in Miguel's jeep found ourselves, as Miguel had promised, in a thriving market. By now we had paired up; myself with Miguel and Andrea with Roman, both of us holding hands as if we had known each other for years. In truth, of course, we hadn't known them for years and knew precious little about either man. Meeting and falling for someone you hardly know is the archetypical holiday romance and was fraught with danger, they could be murderers or conmen for all we knew.

3

MIGUEL

I came from Andalusia, a province of Spain, a region famed for its wide open plains, its orange plantations and vineyards. My family were quite wealthy and were well known and respected in the area. They had a sizeable orange plantation in the foothills of Casarabonela, along with some avocadoes and grape vines. I was my father's right hand man and I helped to manage his business, spending much of my time abroad promoting our wares at trade shows and cultural exhibitions, but I also got my hands dirty from time to time working the land. I am an only child and although I have a cousin, whom my father dotes on, I assumed one day I would inherit the whole estate. My childhood sweetheart, Conchita Gonzales, grew up on the adjacent farm to my father's estate and it was widely expected, by both families that Conchita and I would one day marry, and in doing so the two families businesses would merge to create a powerful force in Andalusia. Conchita's family had grown olives on their plantation for generations and were well regarded by their neighbours and fellow land owners.

Conchita was about five foot nine inches tall and had long powerful strong legs due to riding horses from an early age. She had the most penetrating deep green eyes whose steely gaze, like Medusa, could turn her prey, metaphorically, to stone. She had long, straight, jet-black silky hair and a dark, Mediterranean complexion with a full figure and ample breasts. Her tantalising ruby red lips begged to be kissed. Conchita had a vivacious outgoing personality and a ravenous sexually appetite, she had a reputation for taming the wildest of stallions. Men would look longingly into her smouldering eyes and found themselves under her intoxicating spell. She was so hot it was like instantaneous combustion when she as much as touched her suitors. Her lips, as if plutonium enriched, burnt on contact, she could send a Geiger counter into the red and her penetrating stare was like a laser guided missile.

Conchita and I would ride out together, checking the boundary fences of our estates for damage and would often ride over the dusty plains while galloping alongside each other. I rode an Andalusian Anglo Arab mare, gleaming white, pure as the driven mountain snow and Conchita rode a striking black stallion that most people couldn't tame, but one look from Conchita and the horse knew who was boss. Conchita rode her untamed stallion of the plains like she rode her lover's, using her powerful legs to hold on, with her buttocks clenched tightly to her lovers expanding girth. His pelvic thrusts sending seismic tremors through her quivering, heaving body. The ejaculated fluid surged through her inner sanctum like water that irrigates the fruitful fields that sustain the bountiful crops. Going bareback was dangerous, but she enjoyed the thrill of the Roulette wheel.

The intoxicating scent of orange blossom was ever present in the spring air and burnt our nostrils with its intensity. Astride my pure white mare, like a Gaucho, my gleaming spurs clinking as I rode, I surveyed the land that would, one day, be mine. Whilst out riding alone one day I came upon an isolated hacienda and I could see Conchita's black stallion tethered outside along with a grey mare. I dismounted and tethered my own horse and entered through the doorway of the hacienda. Inside, on a makeshift bed, was Conchita and one of her father's farmhands cavorting. Conchita's fingernails, like tigress claws, gouged deep tracks in her lover's arched back, he groaning in pain and pleasure as he thrust his loins into hers. She looked up and saw me standing there open-mouthed and a big grin spread across her face as she winked at me. "Come and join us darling," she whispered as she pulled back the sheets. I was initially repelled at the thought but something was stirring in my loins and I was unable to resist the urge to mount her and to enter her grand canyon, my silver spurs clinking, as the wild stallion inside of me pounded her trail relentlessly, galloping through my body a stampede of seeds that flooded her fertile valley.

In some ways Conchita and I were soul mates, I was charismatic but egotistical and self-obsessed and she was a seductress who craved continuous male attention and she was impervious to anybody's feelings, her self-gratification was all that mattered. Of course, the men that coupled themselves with her did so knowing that she only wanted uncomplicated sexual gratification without commitment, but that suited most men well enough. In Conchita's mind she was destined to marry me and all the other studs that she shared herself with were a mere sideshow. She didn't think all the cavorting and her gratuitous sexual hijinks would matter a jot to me when it came to my proposing, after all it had long been taken for granted that she and I would marry, if only, to please our respective parents.

One day I had a business meeting in Seville, Andalusia's capital city, and I asked Conchita to accompany me. She could do some shopping while I had my meeting and afterwards we could have lunch together. I intended to broach the subject of betrothal. I was uneasy at the thought of spending the rest of my life entangled in Conchita's web of lies and deceit. I know for certain I wouldn't be able to trust her. Conchita's insatiable lust for sex would make it almost impossible for any one man to satisfy her and I wasn't really convinced of my own sincerity, or indeed, if I really loved her. After my meeting I met Conchita in a pre-arranged spot in the town square. The smell of an open air spice market engulfed our senses and made us salivate with hunger. As we wandered around looking for somewhere to eat we passed the Alcazar Castle complex, built during the Moorish Almohad dynasty, its majestic white walls reflecting the scorching sun. It was early summer and the captivating aroma of sweet scented roses caressed our nostrils and the faint smell of Jasmine would intensify as the evening drew near.

We found a convenient taverna and ordered some sustenance and as Conchita and I shared a bottle of wine the waiter arrived with a huge paella prepared with fresh fragrant ingredients including saffron and a multitude of other spices that tingled our taste buds with delightful flavours. In the distance we could see the spires of the gothic cathedral that was the site of Christopher Columbus's tomb and the famous minaret, turned bell tower, called The Giralda. I looked back nervously into Conchita's deep green eyes and said, "I don't know how to say this but I'm not sure that you and I are right for each other." Conchita's penetrating stare fixed me to the spot.

"What do you mean?" replied Conchita angrily. "How dare you say that, you know our parents wish for us to be married and you've never objected before," Conchita went on.

"Well we've never really had much of a say in the matter," I retorted, "I'm just expected to do what our families wish me to do."

"So who is the bitch?" replied Conchita, her eyes flashing more angrily. "I'll scratch her eyes out." She gestured her outstretched fingers across my face her talon-like nails narrowly missing my chin.

"There is no one else at the moment," I tried to explain, "I just think we should wait and give it more time, don't you agree?" I asked politely. Conchita clearly did not agree as she hurled the now, fortunately, empty paella dish at me with ferocious force. She then stormed off, swearing under her breath. I gave it five minutes before following Conchita into the square hoping she may have cooled her temper down by now. I thought to myself that it was a bit rich, her accusing me of betrayal, when it was she who couldn't keep her knickers on. I knew her various assignations were not serious and were only to quench her thirst for sex, but even so, she had a cheek to storm out on me.

The sun was beginning to set and the aromas of the night filled the humid air; the scent of Jasmine and saffron now lay heavy on the warm gentle breeze which also mingled with the smell of percolating coffee. Soon under a blanket of star spangled sky I could hear the sound of castanets and I could see the famous spectacle of flamenco dancers, their colourful garbs and the rhythm of strumming guitars induced the feeling of passion and suspense. I suddenly caught a glimpse of Conchita dancing flamboyantly in the middle of the square with a group of handsome young men. When she saw me she tossed her head back and stuck out her formidable chest, her low-cut blouse leaving little to the imagination. If she was hoping for a reaction from me she was disappointed as I was unimpressed – after all I'd seen it before, her blatant disregard for modesty. Before too long Conchita hurled her arms around the neck of the nearest man and pulled his head to her heaving breasts, her dark brown nipples showing through her sheer white blouse. The young man began to groan as she rubbed her knee into his groin making him throb with excited anticipation. Conchita dragged the young man through an open gate that led to a walled garden, part of the grounds of the cathedral, the sweet smell of roses and wild flowers filled the air. Conchita and the man trampled carelessly over the neatly arranged flower beds, crushing several prized plants while the other three men followed through the gates to watch. Conchita and their friend cavorting on the manicured lawn of the Cathedral garden.

By now I had seen enough of her antics and I strode purposely through the iron gates and, taking hold of Conchita's arm, dragged her unceremoniously screaming and shouting back to the square. Conchita stood trembling with smouldering rage, hurling abuse and, she was staring straight through me, her eyes on fire like beacons in the night. "Why don't you Vete a la chingada el cabron," Conchita shouted vehemently.

"Pinche puta," I retorted in retaliation, showing I could swear too. Conchita stormed off her head bowed, still muttering to herself. "Pinche punetas" she repeated to herself over and over again as she disappeared in the night. That was the last I saw of Conchita that night, she had made her own way back to her father's ranch. Conchita's explanation of what had taken place when she went to her father in tears, was not quite the same as the true events, she left out the bits that she didn't want him to know about. To her father she was a lovely sweet girl whom everyone adored and he couldn't understand why I had suddenly decided that we were not right for each other. He felt very angry and betrayed.

It wasn't long before he vented his anger to my father, making it very clear that their future business plans would be put on hold until he cajoled me into going ahead with the wedding. My father couldn't apologise enough for my behaviour and assured his long-term friend and prospective business partner that he would speak sternly to me. The next day my father and I had a blazing row, as my father insisted that I made up with Conchita and arrange to marry her as planned, or I'd be disinherited and my position in the business would be in jeopardy. My father was unwilling to listen to any of my protestations of innocence and would not hear a bad word against Conchita.

I stormed off in a rage, I mounted my snowy white mare and galloped off over the plains, riding like the wind it seemed for hours, my poor horse feeling the whip as my frustrations boiled over. I rode on harder and harder until I reached the foothills of the Sierra Nevada and the region of mountain villages known as the Las Alpuja. My horse trotted into the nearest village, both rider and horse by now exhausted.

4

MIGUEL

I led my tired mare to an open water trough where she could quench her thirst, as both myself and my horse were seriously dehydrated due to the intense heat of the midday sun. I entered a small taverna where I could get a drink and something to eat. In the backyard of the taverna they were barbecuing fresh sardines; the aroma created by the crackling pine logs was intoxicating and made my mouth water in anticipation.

Amongst a group of people sitting around the barbecue was a strikingly attractive white woman who I thought wasn't a local. I wandered over and took a seat beside her. I turned and introduced myself to the stunning young woman. "Hi I'm Miguel." I held out my hand in a friendly gesture.

"Hello I'm Jennifer, pleased to meet you," she held out her hand in a limp feminine way. "Have you come for the barbecue," she enquired.

"No, well not particularly," I replied. "I've ridden for quite some miles from my father's orange plantation and just stopped for some refreshment, but the food smelled so good I couldn't resist investigating where the seductive aromas originated from." Jennifer explained that she was staying with her aunt and that she was from England. Her father was quite wealthy and had left her well provided for when he died. Jennifer was tall and slim with pretty blue sequined eyes; she had an assured confidence but had a restrained personality. She was prim and proper in an old fashioned way, she dressed demurely and spoke with an upper class English accent. She had a pale but smooth face, delicate lips and golden brown shoulder-length hair that looked perfectly groomed. I was, by now, captivated by her, she was the exact opposite to Conchita's brash, over the top, extravagant personality. Jennifer was a breath of fresh air and I had to get to know her better. Jennifer wore expensive French perfume, Chanel No. 5; this was her favourite and smelled as heavenly as she looked. She also loved to wear quality designer clothes and elegant high heels by Jimmy Choo. She was in her mid-thirties and although she'd had many boyfriends she'd never found anyone that she could envisage settling down with. Married bliss seemed a condition other people enjoyed but never for her. She certainly was self-confident and always in control of her emotions but she could appear a bit stiff in the typical British tradition and she could seem aloof and disengaged in company, which sometimes soured any relationship that she embarked upon.

Jennifer and I had a long and pleasant chat that lasted into the evening, and after both eating and drinking our fill at the barbecue I suggested a stroll through the village. Arm in arm we set off just in time to see the sun go down, its last rays disappearing behind the mountain ridge. Jennifer's delicate scent hung around our heads as we stared into each other's eyes. I took a huge gulp of air and breathed her in as I took Jennifer's tiny slender hand in mine and kissed it. Jennifer pulled her hand away in shock, she wasn't used to this kind of passion, but she had butterflies in her stomach nonetheless. Bedding Jennifer would not be like making love to Conchita it would require much more finesse. I started to pour my heart out to Jennifer and told her about Conchita's indiscretion and how my father was threatening to disinherit me if I didn't marry my childhood sweetheart. Jennifer was shocked that I had unburdened myself to her when she hardly knew me but she offered me solace. She put her hands to my face and gently kissed me on the lips. Instantly I could feel the human warmth emanating from her, as if being kissed by a fairy queen, an almost magical feeling. Jennifer was like an angel from heaven and Conchita the devil incarnate. As we walked back to where Jennifer's aunt lived we pledged to meet in the morning and to have breakfast together while in the meantime I found a room for the night.

The sun was rising as a cockerel announced its presence noisily. Rubbing the sleep from my eyes I stumbled out of bed and opened the blinds, the rising sun blinding me for a second. I could hardly wait to see Jennifer but first I had a wash but I had nothing to shave with and no change of clothes so I looked dishevelled and smelled musky from the dried perspiration following the long ride the day before. I had bedded my horse down over night and provided her with hay and fresh water. It was time for me to meet Jennifer for breakfast in a pre-arranged café. She was waiting for me at the table-coffee percolating ready to pour. "Good morning, Jennifer," I greeted with a warm accommodating smile. "Good morning to you, Miguel," "Hope you slept well?" Jennifer said enquiringly. We had several cups of coffee and ate a hearty breakfast before leaving hand in hand. "What will you do now?" enquired Jennifer. "Will you go back and apologise to your father and marry Conchita as he wants you to?"

"No, no way", I replied, "I'm not going to apologise and I'm not going to marry Conchita." Jennifer couldn't disguise her relief at hearing my response to her question. She was glad for my own sake if not for hers; no one should be cajoled into a marriage they don't want, she thought to herself, and she couldn't think of anything worse.

For several months I continued to work at my father's plantation but was becoming increasingly disenchanted with my life. I was still seeing Jennifer and had fallen under her spell but, no matter how hard I tried, she would not succeed to my amorous advances. I became frustrated at my failure to bed her and Jennifer's reticence only made me want her more. I conjured up all the charm I could muster but to no avail. One day I awoke and suddenly all became clear in my head, I would ask Jennifer to marry me and that would facilitate access to her knickers and her bank account. On one of my trade conferences I met an Italian called Roman and we had talked at length about starting our own business. We spoke of buying a yacht and trading between the many Caribbean Islands, carrying goods between them. Roman was discontented working for his uncle and had the funds for his part of the venture. If I could convince Jennifer of the merits of our business plans maybe she would lend me the money. I asked Jennifer to go to Barcelona with me for a few days. Jennifer agreed and went shopping for something classy to wear. I booked us into a fabulous hotel, with separate rooms, although if all went well we'd only need one. We spent the first day sightseeing around Barcelona; the towering magnificent cathedral built, as much of Barcelona was, by Gaudi, the famous Spanish architect. I booked a candle-lit table for dinner that evening and concealed in my pocket the eighteen carat gold wedding ring my grandmother left to me. We enjoyed a wonderful meal and had several glasses of wine. The flickering glow of candle light dancing to the hypnotic strains of Rodrigues Guitar Concertos playing in the background, its melancholy lament, pulled at Jennifer's heartstrings. She felt her heart melt, like the dripping candle wax, as she stared into my soft come-to-bed eyes.

I put my hand into my inside pocket and pulled out the wedding ring, leaning across the table I asked Jennifer to marry me. "Oh yes, my darling," was Jennifer's excited reply. She had, at last, got her man. I slipped the ring on her finger to see if it would fit and miraculously it was perfect, I then promised I would buy her the biggest diamond engagement ring the next day. Hand in hand Jennifer and I went up to our bedrooms. "Do I need to sleep alone?" I asked.

"No, silly, we're going to be married," was Jennifer's

answer. "You'll sleep in my bed tonight." Jennifer disrobed and discarded her red dress on the floor. She looked ravishing in her black stockings and suspender belt, pleated frilly knickers and black half-cup push up bra. I flung her onto the bed and I sank to my knees as my tongue caressed Jennifer's honey pot lovingly. I ran my fingers up and down the centre of her arched back inflaming her erogenous zones, my tongue darting in and out, like extracting nectar from an open flower, its delicate pink petals glistening with dew. I mounted my beautiful, cultured blushing bride-to-be and my throbbing girth inside her swelled uncontrollably. Jennifer clasped her groping hands around my buttocks, her perfectly manicured fingernails almost penetrating my skin, as my pelvic thrusts sent her into a frenzied climax. My hands were all over her quivering body, sensually caressing every nerve-tingling inch of her womanly form. I couldn't hold on any longer and after one last rampant surge I was spent. With Jennifer's legs still wrapped round my exuberant body, and cocooned in the white silk sheets, we succumbed to weariness and fell into a deep sleep.

The next morning after a light breakfast I suggested we visit a jewellers, so Jennifer could choose a suitable engagement ring, one I hoped that wouldn't cost too much. After walking up and down the cobbled streets and visiting countless jewellers we found ourselves back at the first shop where Jennifer had spotted a solitaire diamond ring that was simple but elegant, something that matched her couture-culture dress sense. Jennifer looked lovingly into my eyes as I slipped the ring on her finger. I persuaded Jennifer that we shouldn't wait to marry and we should get a special licence and find a local priest who could marry us before the day was at an end. It would be an uncommonly short courtship but I was eager to get my hands on her assets. I also wanted to marry her before my father could talk me out of it; after all, I was partly marrying Jennifer to rebel against my father's wishes. Jennifer resisted, at first, saying that she would prefer to have time to plan what was, after all, the most important day in any woman's life, but I was very persuasive and in the end Jennifer relented and agreed to be married that very day. As I pointed out I had fallen out with my family and Jennifer's father was dead and, apparently, her mother had left the family home when Jennifer was a teenager – she didn't even know the current whereabouts of her mother – so neither of us would have any family to attend the ceremony. After obtaining a marriage licence we scoured the city looking for a priest who would marry us and finally we found a young priest who was prepared to marry us that afternoon. Father Dominic was a progressive priest not too bound by convention.

Jennifer wore a white two-piece designer costume that she already had as there simply wasn't time to find a proper wedding dress, much to her disappointment. I cobbled together an ill fitted suit that looked as if it had just come of the manikin. Jennifer still managed to look sleek and sophisticated in her snug-fitting outfit, her hair and makeup perfectly judged as usual. She wore a delicate shade of pink lipstick and a subtle matching dusky pink eye shadow, a discreet amount of mascara and a little eyeliner to accentuate her eyes. With her posy in her hand she walked up the aisle and stood next to me trembling very slightly. In the absence of a best man, I took my grandmother's antique gold wedding ring out of my pocket and slipped it on Jennifer's finger, to the immortal words of 'now I pronounce you man and wife' from Father Dominic. "You may kiss the bride," Father Dominic exclaimed. Jennifer's lips lingered on mine, it seemed forever, the taste of her lips like nectar on a summer's day. Jennifer and I embraced and then shook Father Dominic's hand warmly. His congratulations and wishes for a long and happy life together were ringing in our ears as we departed the place of sanctuary and Christian worship. I had one last surprise up my sleeve for my blushing bride I had quickly arranged for us to go on our honeymoon to the Caribbean where, I hoped, I would be able to obtain the yacht and lifestyle I'd envisaged. It wasn't just going to be a honeymoon, it would be a whole new life where I wouldn't have to rely on the patronage of my overbearing father.

5

ROMAN

I was born and lived, most of my life, in a small quaint village on the edge of Lake Garda in Italy. Lake Garda has several towns and villages that bordered its shores. Limone, where I grew up, was particularly picturesque with the town's old cobbled streets and alley ways clogged with tourists in the summer, the hustle and bustle of consumers as people shopped for mementoes of their stay in Garda. Limone was quite hilly and afforded fabulous views of Lake Garda. The quickest way to get to Limone was by ferry from Malcesine, which is another quaint little town with narrow winding cobbled streets and a cable car that transported its passengers to a high plateau where impressive vistas could be observed. I left Limone to work for my uncle who owned a large lemon grove near Sorrento. The lemons were used exclusively for the manufacture of Limoncello, a famous tangy liqueur. To start with I learnt the basics from growing and tending the crops to the fermentation process, all the way through to production. Now as a favoured nephew I'd been given an executive position that sounded grander than it was. Basically I was an international rep for the company, tasked with promoting its liqueurs, in all its guises, around the world at trade fairs and such like. Although I had a grand title I was becoming disenchanted with my role and longed for a more rewarding career, maybe one day I'd have my own company.

I was quite good-looking and was never short of female company, however, I had a particular soft spot for a young woman that I'd known from birth, who by coincidence was working and living in Sorrento. Maria Da-Campo was a petite, five foot tall, typical Italian girl. She had lovely big blue eyes and a homely disposition, and she was fairly pretty in an understated way. She was demure and self-denigrating at times, often making jokes about her diminutive stature. She knew that she was a plain-looking girl but still hoped that one day love between her and me would blossom. She found it hard whenever she met up with me as I always had beautiful women flocking around me, although I didn't always reciprocate their amorous advances. I'd had several sexual liaisons but none that led to true romance. Like Romeo, I was looking for my own Juliet, someone that would love me unconditionally.

One day, after returning from an overseas trip, I bumped into Maria in the old town part of Sorrento. I had to look twice as she looked different somehow, I'd never noticed how pretty she really was. Like a beautiful butterfly emerging from the chrysalis, she'd blossomed into a sexy gorgeous young woman with an enigmatic confidence that I hadn't seen before. I noticed, for the first time, the perfume she wore delicate, like freshly cut flowers. Maria's smile, as she saw me, spread across her face, she was pleased to see me again. This could be the beginning of a long romance. After several dates where we kissed and fondled each other I took Maria back to my penthouse apartment in Sorrento old town and there I seduced her and made her feel like a woman for the first time in her life. I took her innocence as our bodies mingled together like molten magma erupting from the centre of the earth I exploding inside her. We lay entwined in each other's arms, like a courting couple frozen in time, as the molten lava spewed from Vesuvius pouring scorn on the inhabitants of Herculaneum.

For a while Maria was ecstatically happy and could envisage a time when she and I would get married and have several bambinos, however in time I came to terms with the fact that I just didn't love Maria enough to marry her and settle down to a life of domesticity. It would, as I endeavoured to explain, be a betrayal that Maria didn't deserve. "I do love you, Maria," I said. "But more like a sister than a lover." These were not the words any woman in love wants to hear. It was like a dagger through her heart.

"I get goose pimples all over my body whenever you run your hands down my back and an intense feeling of delight when your tongue glides over my nipples" Maria explained, "can't you see how much I love you," Maria continued. "When you walk into a room my heart stops and I tremble at the thought of your touch, my darling, please don't leave me now," Maria pleaded.

"I'm so sorry," I replied. "I never meant to hurt you,

my love, but I just don't feel the same as you and you deserve someone who would love you back and give themselves to you completely. I know you don't want to hear this right now," I continued, "but you will find someone who'll be able to make you happy."

I took Maria in my arms for the very last time and kissed her gently on the lips, my hand slipping from her grasp as we parted. Maria wanted a long lingering kiss but I needed to end it there. I didn't want to prolong the agony of jilted love. Maria stood rigidly to the spot, her head bowed and the tears that weld up inside her, now running down her forlorn cheeks. "Don't go," she sobbed as I walked away and closed the door behind me. I decided there and then that now was the time to leave my uncle's employ and strike out on my own. I would get out of Maria's life for good and give her the chance of happiness. I had met and befriended a Spaniard called Miguel on one of my business trips working for my uncle and we had discussed going into business together as we were both disillusioned with our respective careers. It would mean going away to the Caribbean and that would put distance between myself and Maria. It would give Maria a chance to forget me and rebuild her life and, with any luck, in time she would find someone more deserving of her love than I had ever been. I for the first time realised just how lovely Andrea was. At about five foot two inches she was quite petite, especially against my six foot frame. Andrea's long flowing fair hair cascading over her bare, milky-white shoulders. Her deep blue sequined eyes glistened and twitched nervously with anticipation. The serene smile from her rose petal lips brought a warm glow to my heart. We strolled around the market stalls, hand in hand, stopping here and there to barter with the street sellers. The stalls were awash with colour and the air full of wonderful fragrant smells. There were tropical fruits, flowers of many different hues, splendidly coloured love birds in tiny gilt cages waiting to be snapped up by the spellbound tourists looking for objects to fulfil their dull lives.

6

SUSAN

Suddenly Andrea tugged Roman's arm, pulling him into a dilapidated shop doorway. She flung her arms around his neck and kissed him passionately on the lips. Roman reciprocated and found his tongue exploring the delights of Andrea's moist wanton mouth. He pulled her closer to him and she felt his excitement up against her, the passion rising in his blood like Mount Vesuvius ready to explode, a raging tide of emotions swept through his veins. Andrea felt a tingle in the pit of her stomach, an aching desire for copulation. Roman had aroused the woman in Andrea; the genie was out of the bottle and she could not put the cork back in, indeed she did not want to. All this time the myriad of tourists just bustled their way by, disregarding, or merely not noticing, the debauchery before their eyes. Roman's hands caressed Andrea's erogenous zones making her gasp with pleasure. Andrea decided that perhaps now was not the time or place to go all the way to paradise with Roman, so, grasping his hand, they ran through the crowds, laughing and giggling like teenagers. Just up ahead they could see Miguel and I meandering along, hand in hand, seemingly without a care in the world. Oblivious to those around us, we only had eyes for each other. Roman and Andrea quickly caught up with us.

After a short discussion about how we should spend the rest of the day, we decided it was time to head for one of the white sandy beaches that festooned the island. There was a tourist beach just outside of the village with all the usual trappings; copious water sport activities, numerous umbrellas to shelter beneath from the unrelenting sun and lilos scattered over the white expansive beach. However, about three kilometres north of the village, Miguel had found a small, quiet, sheltered bay, a haven only known to the locals. It was a bit off the beaten track and you could only get down to it with a four wheel drive vehicle as the terrain was very unforgiving. It was a bit of a bumpy ride but it proved to be worth the discomfort. This was more like the tranquil, scenic, serene vision of paradise that had populated Andrea's creative images. This was my version of nirvana. Brilliant white soft sand, unspoilt by the tourist trade, tall slender palm trees swaying in the gentle warm fragranced tropical breeze. We all collapsed on the beach and sank into the scorching white sand, our bodies almost devoured.

Miguel and I were laying in a warm embrace; Miguel captivated by my deep green eyes and I swooned with unadulterated lust for Miguel, whilst Roman and Andrea just lay together peering above their heads into the majestic blue expanse of the Caribbean sky. As Andrea turned her head to glance into Roman's eyes she felt a sense of calm waft over her, the like of which, she had not felt since the days she spent at her aunt's cottage in the heart of the Yorkshire Dales. It was a welcome change from the dark dismal existence that she had to endure in Hartlepool. Andrea's thoughts slipped back in time, she somehow missed the countryside and the somewhat guarded warmth of its inhabitants. Andrea recounted just how quickly winter seemed to creep upon them. She would lay each night, her nose pressed against the window pane, gazing across the open fields that once lay shimmering with an evergreen lustre, now laying glistening under a blanket of ice-encrusted snow, sheltering beneath a lunar lantern and gleaming jewels above. The winter months seemed to pass so slowly, but before she knew it spring had arrived.

Andrea awoke one morning to a lit room, aglow like the eye of heaven. She gazed through the lattice window, there to greet her was the sun in all its glorious brilliance, perched upon the horizon like an orange suspended in space. For a while her vision was impaired by the brilliance of the sun's iridescent glowing mass, but all shadows were soon to pass from her mind as she sprang out of her bed like a mischievous young hare gasping with exuberance and intent on getting her first breath of the clean crisp spring air. As Andrea peered above she noticed a solitary lark winging its way skyward, its joyous song refreshed her ears and for a while her head swam with its sweet soaring music. She looked down at her feet and saw a young rabbit scampering off across the field and watched as it eventually disappeared from sight into the evergreen hedgerow. The fields, it seemed, stretched forever as far as the eye could see. The sweet smell of the grass filled her lungs as she took a long deep breath.

Andrea loved this countryside with an insatiable lust, like a woman infatuated with a man. She ran through the long grass and stabbed her hands out to touch the knee-high daisies that grew in random clusters all around. Andrea ran like a demented dog, not knowing where her legs would take her next. At last she became weary and collapsed to the ground, holding her head and rolling in the long cool grass. She wondered in bewilderment at this beautiful new day. As Andrea now lay tranquil and calm on this Barbados beach she realised she had to put thoughts of her past, however reassuring and comforting it may be, behind her and concentrate on the present. She could, after all, be about to embark upon the most important relationship of her life. She felt that this could be more significant than a mere holiday romance.

It was cool and peaceful under the shadow of the palm tree's outstretched branches, but I was eager to leap into the warm, sensuous blue water that seemed to gently caress the shore. "Come on, Andrea," I yelled as I ran towards the oncoming waves, "let's get wet." Neither of us had our bathing costumes on, as we had dressed for sightseeing, however, apart from ourselves the beach was practically deserted.

"Okay I'm coming," replied Andrea. We clasped hands and entered the swirling water together. The first wave took Andrea's breath away; we splattered and giggled as another wave lifted us of our feet dunking us under the water. Miguel and Roman dived in just as I popped up from beneath the waves, my fulsome bosom heaving beneath my sodden skimpy top that had now become very see-through. As Andrea surfaced it became clear that her top too had become rather more revealing. Roman offered Andrea his shirt to cover her embarrassment, but Miguel could only ogle my sumptuous breasts.

Miguel stood behind me and gently, almost tentatively, ran his hands over my erect nipples, feeling the fullness of my breasts. I showed no signs of objecting so Miguel's fondling became more robust. Before long our bodies could be seen entangled and gyrating on the edge of the surf. The sight of Miguel and I copulating at the water's edge enflamed Roman's passions to the point where he could control himself no longer. Roman took Andrea to heights beyond anything she had experienced before, as beneath the shade of the swaying palms, they joined together consummating in a simultaneous climax of love and passion that sent volcanic tremors through Andrea's taut body. Exhausted and spent we all lay beneath the shade of the palms and drifted off to sleep. By the time we awoke it was late afternoon.

"I think it's time we were getting back to the hotel," I said to Andrea in a hushed voice.

Miguel overheard, "Sure we will take you back whenever you wish, but why don't you come back with Roman and me and we can show you round our yacht and you could stay for dinner?"

"Well that's very kind of you, Miguel," I answered, "but we need to get cleaned up and we need a change of clothes."

"Well that's okay, we will stop at your hotel, pick up a

change of clothes and you can shower and change on the yacht." Miguel nodded to Roman and Roman gestured back that he was in agreement. Roman suggested that they could stay the night and return to the hotel the next morning.

The yacht was moored in a secluded little bay less than an hour's drive from the hotel. The thought of spending a night of passion with Miguel was too much for me to pass up. Andrea was by now besotted with Roman, but all the same she felt a little more apprehensive than I. However, after a bit of persuasion from me she agreed to go back to the yacht and to spend the evening and night with Miguel and Roman.

7

It was very early evening when we arrived at the secluded bay where Miguel and Roman's yacht was moored. It was moored some one hundred metres off shore and it necessitated the use of a rowing boat to attain access to it.

"I thought you said it was a modest yacht?" I enquired.

"It looks quite regal from here."

"Well perhaps we were a bit economical with the truth, but I didn't want to sound too flash in case it put you off."

"I suppose I can forgive you this once," I replied, "Has your yacht got a name?" I asked.

"Yes indeed," answered Miguel, "she is called Silver Mist. She is very sleek and is one of the fastest yachts around these islands," he boasted.

Andrea and I climbed aboard the rowing boat and held on tight as Miguel and Roman pushed off from the beach. Soon Miguel and Roman were pulling feverishly on the oars drawing them ever closer to Silver Mist. As they drew alongside we could see for the first time the full extent of the yacht's magnificence.

The vessel had a long, sleek, streamlined hull, its tall rakish masts piercing through the silky blue sky above. It just lay there with an eerie silence, gently bobbing up and down on the rippling tide, glistening white like a precious jewel in the sun. Roman held the rope ladder still while Andrea and I scaled the side of Silver Mist. Once on board we were surprised to see a huge white marble table surrounded by deck chairs and sun loungers. A large umbrella protruding from out of the centre of the oval marble table offered some welcome shade from the awesome suns' rays. Andrea and I were surprised to see the table was already set for dinner. Copious amounts of fresh tropical fruits decorated the table, and an ice bucket containing a magnum of champagne, appropriately chilled, was waiting to be uncorked. There were four place settings adorned with silver cutlery and neatly folded serviettes. An ostentatious silver candelabra with three long red candles, was, at present, unlit. Miguel and Roman laughed as they welcomed us aboard Silver Mist.

"I meant to tell you that we have a comrade who looks after us on our voyages," explained Miguel rather sheepishly. "Gideon does all our cooking and helps out on board the yacht. If you would like to follow Roman he will show you to your cabins for the night and show you where the shower room is. I am afraid it is a communal shower, we all share here."

"Thank you," I replied, "I am sure we will be very comfortable and I do not mind who I share the shower with." I gave a wry smile and winked at Roman, who escorted us below deck. Andrea stared at me with disdain;

how dare I give Roman 'the come on' with my licentious come-to-bed eyes. Below deck the accommodation was surprisingly palatial; the cabin that we shared had all the conveniences we could wish for. There was en-suite toilet and washbasin, and two single beds fully made up, the corners of the sheets neatly tucked in.

Andrea slipped out of her soiled, sweaty garments and was the first to meander along the corridor to the shower room. She had a long exhilarating shower that left her feeling refreshed and replenished after the dusty hot day. By the time Andrea had returned to the cabin I had disrobed and was keen to wash away the excesses of the day. As I made my way to the shower I bumped into Roman coming the opposite way. I wiggled my sexy frame as I squeezed past him. "I don't suppose you would like to scrub my back, would you, Roman," I asked teasingly, intimating that I would not be adverse to a close encounter in the shower.

"I would gladly wash your back for you, Susan, but I am not sure Andrea will approve," Roman replied.

"Well don't tell her then," I winked and beckoned Roman tantalisingly thrusting my breasts in his face. It was hard for any man to repel my advances once I had decided I wanted his attention. It was the hottest cold shower I had ever had, my skin tingled, not from the cold water, but with excitement. My cold shower assignation with Roman was just pure lust and when Roman's thrusting body shuddered to a halt I just smiled serenely and showered the evidence of our infidelity away. Roman felt guilty, but I was unrepentant about my disloyalty towards my friend.

I didn't realise that Andrea was gradually falling in love with Roman and, indeed, Roman too was feeling the pangs of love, which made him feel even more disgusted with himself for what he and I had just done. It was all very well for me to dismiss the importance of our furtive copulations in the shower but Roman felt as if he had plunged a knife into Andrea's heart. It was so easy for me to wash the evidence down the drain and to smile as if nothing had happened. Roman and I dried ourselves and our eyes did not meet again until we were sat round the dinner table with Miguel and Andrea. I sat down, still smirking to myself inwardly but outwardly I came across as demure and almost angelic-like. "So what's for dinner?" I asked. "I'm starving, I think I have worked up quite an appetite." I stared Roman in the eyes and grinned shamefully. Just as Miguel was about to answer Gideon came on deck bearing our starters. A tiger prawn cocktail brimming with a rich Rose Marie sauce and adorned with a salad dressing. Gideon served the starters and poured out the chilled champagne. We all chinked our glasses in a toast, before savouring the delights of Gideon's cooking.

"So what would you two lovely ladies like to do tomorrow," asked Roman. "We could take you back to your nice comfortable hotel or you could come with us on a cruise round the islands."

Andrea and I looked across the table at each other and Andrea could see the excitement in my bulging eyes. "I think we should really go back to the hotel," Andrea replied, "but your offer is very tempting. We wouldn't want to get in your way or disrupt your business venture." I raised my eyebrows at this.

"I don't think they would ask us if that were likely," I quipped, "and in any case, don't I get a say in this."

"Of course you do I just thought that we might,"–

"Might what?" I interrupted. "Have too much fun, you mean? Well I don't know about you, Andrea darling, but that's what I am here for." Andrea smiled demurely and succumbed to my will once more.

"Okay so that's a date then," I laughed. We ate our starters and were soon wading through the main course of lobster, freshly caught and cooked to perfection by Gideon with loving care. He was proud of the gastronomic delights that he could conjure up. We sat there gorging ourselves on the fruits of Gideon's efforts and after a sweet lavish pudding all four of us were comfortably satisfied.

We sat around for the rest of the evening chatting and sipping cocktails, and yet another bottle of champagne. The champagne bubbles fizzed up my nose and made me giggle uncontrollably. Miguel suggested a stroll around the deck as I was becoming inebriated and Andrea was decidedly tipsy. All four of us took a stroll round the deck to walk off the effects of all that food and drink. By now it was late evening and the majestic sun's rays had finally disappeared from view and the deep red glowing mass disappeared below the horizon. The stars began to appear in the night sky, like light bulbs being switched on by some unseen hand, one by one across the velvet black sky. Miguel and I said goodnight to Andrea and Roman, as we staggered down below deck fondling each other feverishly. Roman and Andrea stayed on deck and strolled, hand in hand, for another turn round the deck.

The silky canopy, studded with brightly lit stars, seemed to be dimmed by the brilliance of Andrea's gleaming eyes. As Roman took Andrea in his arms her heart began to float like a hot air balloon on a thermal, rising with breathless speed. Her head felt as if she had been drinking champagne all night, such was the mist that swirled about in her mind.

Roman's warm, sensuous touch felt like the warm glow she had inside, as the day's sunshine, like slender fingers of moulded bronze, caressed her smooth, soft, angelic face. As his lips touched hers she could feel her heart pounding inside her chest and the surge of emotion rushed through her throbbing body. As they stared simultaneously into the dark expanse of infinity they revelled in the sure knowledge that they were undeniably in love. Soon Roman and Andrea were locked in an intimate embrace pulling feverishly at each other's clothes and ravishing their pulsating bodies, like a highwayman lying in wait. Roman plundered her heart her mind and her body, he took all the jewels she had to give. They fell with gay abandonment into an open lifeboat and it did not take too long to discard their clothes. Roman was all over her, gorging himself on her young succulent flesh as he lay between her milk white heaving breast. Making love in a lifeboat in the open sultry sea air heightened their lust for each other. Seagulls that had disappeared from the night sky seemed to miraculously reappear to make one last sortie round their heads, their shrill boisterous cries almost urging Roman on as his pelvis moved in rhythm with their beating wings and Andrea's beating heart.

Sea spray covered their heaving bodies as Roman's hips jerked for the last time, sending a shuddering stream of delight through Andrea's exultant wanton body.

The two lovers held each other in an embrace, entwined together. Lovingly, Roman gently caressed Andrea's silk-like face with the tender touch of a man in love. Under the watchful eyes of the full silvery moon, Roman and Andrea sank into a blissful deep slumber.

8

Miguel and I awoke and made our way to the top deck, where Andrea and Roman were still fast asleep, Andrea's legs wrapped around Roman's naked torso. "Come on you two its time you were up." I bent down to give Andrea a helping hand. "So you spent the night up here did you? I thought I didn't hear you come to bed last night. I hope you two had as much fun as Miguel and I did, although, to be honest, it is all a bit of a blur this morning.

"I'm not surprised," retorted Andrea, "after what you had to drink last night." I hiccupped just then, reinforcing Andrea's view that I had overdone things a bit last night.

"This sun is hell already," I exclaimed, "I'm going to take my clothes off and dive into that lovely still blue water. Who is coming in with me?" Roman rubbed the sleep from his eyes and gazed over the side of the yacht. "I guess an early dip will wake me up" said Roman.

We all agreed that it would be great fun to have a swim before sitting down for breakfast. Andrea peered over the port side and instantly yelped with delight as she spotted a shoal of dolphins darting in and out of the water, leaping playfully into the warm expanding air. We watched as the dolphins disappeared beneath Silver

Mist's hull. Andrea dashed over to the starboard side to witness them reappear from under the hull.

Suddenly the dolphins leapt right out of the water and Andrea could appreciate the true majesty of these wonderful creatures. As the dolphins dived back into the deep blue aqua they sent up a fountain of cold salty water that rained down upon all four of us. It was time to enter into the inviting calm waters. Holding hands both couples jumped over the side together. As Andrea immersed herself in the silky blue oceanic garden of nature's creation, she caught sight of a gigantic sunfish; the overwhelming grace with which it lazily carved its passage through the warm sensuous aqua, left her breathless. She dived down deeper and deeper into the desert-like expanse of the inviting sea, as she did so, she left Roman floundering in her wake. Andrea could only wonder and marvel at the sight of such beauty. The sea was a hive of activity with its myriad forms of life. The colours of the coral, their tentacles swaying with the motion of the water, were awe inspiring and left her heart a flutter like the beating wings of a fleeting butterfly. She allowed herself to gently float up the watery steps of the sea's spiralling staircase and broke the surface to the rapturous applause of the never diminishing seagulls, their noise and exuberance attacked her head like a battering ram after the serene embrace of the tranquil blue desert-like expanse of the Caribbean Sea. She could not help wondering what kind of mood mothers nature was in when she created such beauty that, not even the perfection of the artist's brush could imitate. Andrea looked up to see the others splashing about playfully on the surface, as Miguel continued to be excited at the sight of my bulbous breasts pushed up against his hairy chest.

Gideon lent over the side of the yacht and called to Miguel, Breakfast is served and there are towels over the deckchairs for you." At this, Miguel and Roman climbed aboard Silver Mist, they held out their hands to assist Andrea and myself to climb aboard. We dried ourselves and put on some clothes before tucking into a full English breakfast and drank copious amounts of freshly squeezed orange juice. After a short while Miguel decided it was time to up anchor and to set sail so he could show us girls how well she handled. The clap from the canvas as the wind struck the sails full on made Andrea jump. In no time at all Silver Mist was carving a swathe through the silky blue water, gathering speed relentlessly. She was how Miguel had described her, very sleek and fast. "Set sail for St. Lucia," commanded Miguel to Gideon, who had now hung up his chef's hat and become a jolly tar. As they left the shelter of the tranquil bay the waves began to crash upon Silver Mists' bows, but she just cut through them, like a knife through butter.

Andrea and Roman lay next to each other, soaking up the golden rays of sun that were gently warming their bodies. Andrea had gone from a pale white complexion to a glowing bronze goddess. These last couple of days had been a revelation to Roman, who up to now had thought of himself as the archetypical bachelor, free and single. When he looked at Andrea her eyes were like a burst of interstellar starlight, her smile like a jewelled moon beaming across her angelic face. Although they had not known each other very long he was sure he had fallen in love with Andrea. He could not recall ever feeling this way about any other woman that he had previously met, and there had been quite a few, it felt as if he had known Andrea all his life. She was like the proverbial breath of fresh air, all of the natural beauty of nature personified, she smelt like wild flowers whose scent hung in the breeze. There was nothing artificial or contrived or cultivated in her serene smile, her skin was soft, like silk, her lips, with a satin lustre, begged to be kissed.

Miguel and I just laughed and chatted as we were larking about on the deck, play fighting like teenage lovers. Miguel was overjoyed at his good fortune in meeting me; the sex was truly scintillating and I was quite unlike any woman he had known. Miguel had been married once and had seriously fallen out with his estranged wife. He promised himself that he would never allow himself to become trapped like that again. It was late afternoon when we reached the shady lagoon just off shore. St. Lucia was a small haven, a beautiful, sparsely populated island that remained unspoilt by the ravages of time or human contamination.

Miguel dropped the anchor and waited for the splash as Gideon pulled down the sails. The anchor took hold and Silver Mist was once again harnessed to the oceans' floor. The warm clear waters of the secluded bay lured Andrea and I, as if beckoning us, to enter into its glorious sublime caressing waters. We had landed on the most deserted part of the island away from the throng and happy partying tourists that swelled the islands population at this time of the year. The two of us swam gracefully towards the welcoming shore, less than one hundred yards away. Andrea looked back to see Roman and Miguel enter the water with a splash, the two men caught up quickly and we all reached the shore at the same time. My feet sank into the soft warm white sand as I dragged myself to the shelter of a cluster of palm trees, whose roots clung tantalisingly to the extreme edge of the shore, fighting a rear guard action against erosion and the ravages of time. Andrea picked her way nimbly and skilfully around some flotsam that had been washed upon the beach in one of the frequent tropical storms that pounded the islands remorselessly and with unrelenting ferocity.

Miguel and Roman were soon lying beside Andrea and I, resting beyond the glare of the tropical sun beneath the outstretched branches of the palm trees. The late afternoon air was full of the scent of fragrant pine forests that festooned the hillside above the beach, mixed with azalea trees and the lingering smell of nutmeg and other spices that combined to make a heady cocktail of aromas. Roman put his hand out to Andrea and, helping her to her feet, they both went for a stroll along the beach, Andrea's hand clasped tightly in his own. It was nice to have a bit of privacy away from Miguel and I. Roman wanted to discover all he could about Andrea's life, what made her happy and what made her sad. He had not had the time, yet, to unravel her past or to delve deeper into her psyche, such was the acceleration of their exhilarating whirlwind romance. When Roman and Andrea made love the earth truly moved, but at other times, he felt that

Andrea could become detached sometimes staring into infinity her eyes glazed over and seemingly in a world of her own. Roman just wanted to be part of that secret world that Andrea would psychologically escape to when she entered into this hypnotic state.

Andrea, for her part, had fallen so deeply in love with Roman that she had barely given any thought to his life prior to their meeting and had not contemplated how his past life might have any bearing on their future together, she just revelled in the moment. She drank in the atmosphere of every moment that they had spent together, each sultry kiss, every sensual caress of her neck and all the softly spoken words of love that fell upon her eager ears, were stored in her mind in case she never experienced such depths of passion again. There was an inbuilt insecurity that had insidiously crept into her life leaving her feeling vulnerable and fragile. She almost expected to be hurt in any relationship that she embarked upon, such was the emotional scarring that had left her damaged so badly after her years of neglect and sexual molestation by her violent drunken father; it was not easy to cast aside the emotional shackles of her past. She could never forgive her mother for looking the other way while her vile father violated her virginal young body, leaving her with a legacy of guilt and frigidity. Even her sexual assignations with Uncle Eric were a consequence of her early years of molestation, she thought it her duty to be submissive to older men like Uncle Eric. She had certainly overcome her fear of intimacy with Roman, he was such a gentle and considerate lover.

When Andrea looked deep into Roman's eyes it was

as if she was entering another world and all the pain of the past was obliterated. It was like being submerged in a tranquil pool of warm sensuous water or floating weightlessly on a cotton wool cloud. Sometimes she would get palpitations just holding his hand, she had never before experienced such depths of physical pleasure and fulfilment that Roman had given her. But sometimes she felt like she was on the periphery of reality looking in upon herself, she felt she needed to transcend the boundaries of her own imaginations, to make that leap from the darkness and turbulence of despair to the wonderful, warm, enveloping, glowing warmth of love. Andrea knew very little about Roman; she knew that he was Italian and come from a small village outside Naples and that he came from a wealthy and privileged background but he had told her nothing of significance about his personal life, nor indeed, how he and Miguel had met. Their business venture seemed to be shrouded in secrecy, they would only say that they dealt in commodities of some considerable value. To be honest Andrea nor I cared how they made their money, it was their business and we did not wish to intrude.

Miguel and I were playfully rolling around in the shimmering white sands, fondling each other with an urgency that suggested we were becoming aroused. At that point, Andrea looked up to see the beginning of what looked like a storm approaching. "Hey you two" she yelled, "stop the foreplay and cast your eyes on the horizon. Is it my imagination or are we about to have a storm," she asked. Miguel and Roman looked up at once.

"Yes I think you're right." answered Miguel. "We had

better get back to the yacht as soon as possible." We all got into the rowing boat that Miguel had previously moored on the shore and paddled for all our worth. Severe storms can hit suddenly in these tropical parts and there was no time to lose. We needed to reach the relative safety of Silver Mist quickly as the dark foreboding clouds had almost engulfed Silver Mist in an inky blackness, as if someone had eclipsed the sun with a huge blanket. Suddenly the gentle breeze had turned into a howling wind that chilled us to the bone. We shivered as we toiled against the elements, the sea now erupting into a cauldron of despair, we battled on feverishly against the raging torrent and eventually managed to clamber aboard Silver Mist with a helping hand from Gideon. "Thank God you have got back safely. I was beginning to think you were not going to make it," Gideon said frantically. "I feared we would be swamped by one of those huge waves and all be swept overboard to our deaths," exclaimed Miguel. "Come on, girls, let's get into some dry clothes and get ourselves warmed up," said Miguel.

"Yes," interrupted Roman, "you are shivering and your skin is covered in goose pimples, you will catch your death," Roman exclaimed, looking lovingly into Andrea's deep blue eyes. They went below deck to have a shower and dry off before changing into some dry clothes.

By now Silver Mist was lurching from side to side being buffeted on all sides by the swirling winds and crashing waves. Miguel, Roman and their solitary crew member decided that the best course of action would be to remain anchored where they were and to try and weather the storm. The relative safety of the sheltered cove, would they hoped, afford them some protection from this catastrophic maelstrom that had engulfed us. The storm raged on until darkness fell when, all at once, an eerie silence came upon us making everyone feel somehow uneasy, as if something untoward was about to happen. We took advantage of the sudden calm and sat down to some supper all washed down with copious amounts of alcohol, enough to get me giggling as I staggered below deck. I emerged ten minutes later clutching what looked like a games board. "Look what I have found hidden in my cabin," I announced. "It's an Ouija Board." There was stunned silence. "Come on, let's all sit round the table and hold hands," I said insistently, "It will be a laugh."

"I don't think that would be a good idea," opined Miguel, "you shouldn't play with the dark side."

I, however, was now even more intrigued and became ever more insistent that I got my way, and reluctantly Miguel and Roman agreed. Andrea still had reservations about meddling with things that were beyond her comprehension, but she gave in to me, because that is what you did with me, if you wanted a quiet life. We sat round the table on deck in the open air, now that the storm had passed, that had the familiar warmth and fragrance of the Caribbean. I spread the board upon the table and Andrea put an upturned glass in the middle, we all put their hands on the glass and almost immediately it began to mysteriously move; an ice-cold shiver ran through Andrea's body. "God, it feels like someone has just walked over my grave," Andrea screamed. "I don't like this."

"Don't be silly," I replied, "someone is moving the glass." She looked at Miguel accusingly.

"Don't blame me," Miguel gulped, "I told you not to dabble in the unknown, didn't I?" At this point the glass shuddered violently and began to move across the board, it appeared to be spelling out a name: J.E.N.N.Y. The glass came abruptly to a halt.

"Who is Jenny," I asked. They all shook their heads.

"I don't know," replied Miguel, "I've never met anyone called Jenny."

"No, nor me," exclaimed Roman. But Gideon, who had just finished clearing away after supper, looked at Miguel with a menacing glare that suggested that he was not telling the truth. Fortunately no one noticed Gideon's look of disdain. I remained oblivious to any secrets harboured by Miguel. We all agreed that we had had enough excitement for one night and decided it was time to retire to our cabins for a good night sleep.

Andrea and Roman could hear Miguel and I making love noisily in the next cabin but, Roman, although intoxicated by Andrea's body, could not help falling fast asleep. Andrea tried desperately to sleep but, even though silence had long since replaced the rumbustious love making coming from our cabin, she couldn't drift off. She was feeling very claustrophobic in the stifling heat of the cabin; there was just no air down there. She blindly made her way to the deck, stumbling over some old rope that was heavy with the smell of hemp. She collapsed onto a sunbed and gazed up at the stars that shone with an intense glow. The tranquillity was broken by a far-off clap of thunder and a streak of lightning that flashed across the distant horizon, suggesting the imminent return of the previous storm. Andrea put her hands over her eyes, peering through her fingers, she always felt uneasy with lightning since she was a little girl.

Sure enough the claps of thunder and flashes of bright red streaks that lit up the night sky were getting ever closer and between the claps of thunder the eerie silence engulfed her senses. All she could hear was the gentle howling of the wind through the rigging that seemed to echo a garbled warning of imminent danger and the sound of the waves crashing against Silver Mist's hull. Suddenly Andrea felt very cold and intimidated as if she was not alone; she could almost sense a presence of someone or something lurking in the shadows in the pitch black of the night and she felt like she was walking all alone through a graveyard. Alone, that is, apart from the spirits that surreptitiously hovered behind the gravestones, lying in wait to trap any mortal foolish enough to enter into the dark underworld inhabited by ghouls and restless spirits. By now the far off rumble of thunder had crept ever closer until a crescendo of crashes savaged her head with the ferocity of a jackhammer. Out of the deathly darkness a sheet of blinding lightning tore across the horizon to illuminate the night sky and reveal for the first time, to her horror, what appeared to be a shadowy figurehead covered by a cloak. All Andrea's senses tingled as she was rooted to the spot; she could smell the stench of something long dead and not of this world, like an unearthed corpse crawling with maggots, a seething heaving wreck of undiluted evil. Only a scattering of light emanating from the partly obscured moon managed to trickle down after the flashes of lightning had diminished. By now the shadowy figure had disappeared and Andrea wondered if she had imagined everything. Andrea groped her way back to the cabin where Roman slept undisturbed throughout her ordeal.

She cuddled up close to the man she was falling in love with, her clammy palms seizing his outstretched hand, she needed the reassuring comfort from feeling the pulsing of blood through Roman's veins. She felt herself slipping into a deep sleep. Now rose-tinted dreams engulfed her senses and she was transported far away to a distant time and place where her inhibitions and self-doubt vanished without trace, a serenity came over her with a satisfyingly warm glow. She imagined her and Roman alone on a deserted island, its white, luminous, shimmering sands sculptured out of the sea, her lips and his melted together under the scorching sun their bodies entwined. She entrusted herself in his manly arms, his soft touch, his gentle caress that made her groan with delight, she gave herself willingly to Roman's lustful craving. Like a coconut exploding, his man milk erupted, covering her childbearing motherhood. With an inner roar and gravitas of Mount Vesuvius she succumbed to his will in heavenly rapture.

9

As the storm returned with renewed vigour Andrea's dreams of warm sensual passion were rudely interrupted as Silver Mist violently started to sway from side to side catapulting Andrea and Roman out of their bunks, sending them unceremoniously to the cabin floor. Silver Mist had succumbed to the rigours of the ferocious storm wrenching her from her overnight moorings; the anchor torn from the seabed. The yacht was cast adrift in the swirling maelstrom that threatened to engulf us, bobbing up and down helplessly in the wild raging sea, like a ping pong ball out of control and in freefall. Andrea and Roman rummaged about in the dark, finding some clothes to adorn themselves with. "Are you all right Andrea?" enquired Roman, his voice quivered with concern.

"Crap I think I hit my head on something hard" Andrea exclaimed, dabbing her hand to her head feeling for signs of blood. "I think I'm okay and I don't think I have cut my head. Are you okay," Andrea enquired of Roman.

"Yes I'm fine, Andrea my darling, I think we'd better make our way on deck to see what has happened and see if Miguel and Susan are okay," Roman replied.

Roman and Andrea made their way on deck to find Miguel and I already there. Miguel was grappling with the helm, trying to impose some kind of control over the yacht. It was an almost impossible task as Silver Mist was being buffeted by mountainous waves that crashed mercilessly against her hull. Miguel was almost washed overboard as her stern was hit by an enormous wave. Roman rushed to help his friend, clasping his hand, preventing him from tipping over the side.

"Shit," I exclaimed. "I thought we were going to lose you," my voice quivered.

"What's going to happen to us, are we going to capsize?" asked Andrea in a fevered distraught voice.

"No, no, do not worry, we'll be fine," replied Miguel, "the old girl has been in worse scrapes before, we'll just sit out the storm and wait for the weather to break."

"I'm afraid it's going to be a bit uncomfortable for a while," added Roman. The yacht continued to roll from side to side as now heavy rain lashed into our faces. "Where the hell is Gideon, he should be helping you," I said.

"Yes you are right, I would have thought he would be the first on deck," replied Miguel.

"I will go and look for him," interrupted Roman.

Roman entered Gideon's cabin only to find it empty and subsequently discovered that he was nowhere to be found on board. Roman and Miguel had to come to the conclusion that Gideon must have been washed overboard before they had arrived on deck. As there was no sign of him it had to be the only explanation. The poor man must have perished whilst we slept. Now the four of us were on our own against the elements. The once calm and tranquil sea had erupted into a swirling whirlpool of living hell. The ghostly early morning sky was devoid of any sunlight, only dark, dismal, menacing clouds populated the horizon as far as the eye could see and above our heads a thick blanket of dense black cloud threatened to extinguish any remaining light. The darkness fell upon us like a matador's cloak over the bull's head, quiet and motionless we awaited the kill. The fear between all four of us was palpable; there was a sense of foreboding that was hard to ignore. We huddled together for warmth and comfort and prayed we could ride out the storm. The wind howled around the main mast and the rain lashed down upon us, the sound of hailstones hitting the deck, reminiscent of the restless beating of Andrea's heart. There was a spine-tingling mournful sound that seemed to emanate from the rigging as the roaring wind continued its haunting melody. The conditions continued to deteriorate. The incessant hailstone beating our hands and faces raw, with its intensity, all hell would ensue over the next twelve hours until at last the storm broke. In the meantime the four of us had hidden under a tarpaulin for shelter and had succumbed to the temptation to go to sleep, exhausted by our endeavours to survive.

10

MIGUEL

As I slept I dreamt about my dark past and the shameful secrets that I had buried in my subconscious, some of the things I had done were too hideous even to admit to myself. I was full of guilt and remorse but that did not negate my evil actions or the destructive hatred of my former wife. I had intimated that my wife Jennifer had perished after falling overboard and although there were exhaustive searches by the authorities her body was never found. This was, of course, a complete fabrication. I knew exactly what had happened to my wife and was haunted by it to this day. I had married Jennifer for her money, indeed, I would not have his lavish life style or my beloved yacht Silver Mist if it were not for her benevolence. I ran my own business supplying goods to the West Indian Islands – spices and consumables – but it was not that profitable. In an attempt to free myself from my wife's purse strings I became involved in drug smuggling. Running drugs between the Caribbean Islands proved far more lucrative. Things took a more sinister twist when I started visiting the island of Haiti. I found myself entangled in the satanical rituals and barbaric practices that had persisted over centuries. Jennifer had discovered the truth about my business and was threatening to expose my drug-running activities to the police. I pleaded with her, but, it was no use, Jennifer was a very moralistic self-righteous woman who could not be swayed once her mind was made up. I really had no choice, as I saw it, she had to go.

I researched ways in which I could get rid of my nauseas wife and came up with the idea of plying her with an old Haitian poison supplied by the local witch doctor, then I acquired the services of some unscrupulous locals who regularly carried out satanic ritual killings, to assist me in my wife's murder. I arranged for my wife a sumptuous feast aboard my yacht so I could secrete the poison; it was a drug that slows the heartbeat to the point of near-death, the victim showing all the external appearances of being dead, their pulse would be undetectable. Jennifer foolishly assumed I was merely laying on a feast and was trying to construct some kind of reconciliation between us, although she suspected it was a plan to persuade her not to go to the authorities and to secure her silence. She was unaware that I planned to silence her for good! We sat down together, eyes fixed across the table, the meal prepared by my own hand; I had given my cook the night off so I could be alone with Jennifer. The food looked sumptuous and inviting but hid its deadly secret well. "If you think that a lovely meal, glowing candles and a romantic evening is going to buy my silence, my darling, you are very much mistaken," said Jennifer, "but I'll eat with you as you have gone to such trouble, after all, it might be the last we share together." Jennifer carried on, "Look at it in biblical terms like a last supper," she laughed sarcastically. I just smiled to myself. A last supper indeed, I mused, but for who? Jennifer tucked into the main course and guzzled back the chilled wine as I looked on, gleefully awaiting the moment when the secret infusion will have done its work.

I did not have long to wait, Jennifer began to slip into an induced comatose state, her eyelids fixed open, her breathing almost non-existent. Her body was frozen paralysed, unable to move; her lips were unable to speak and yet her mind was alert and she could hear and see all that was about to happen to her. I hurried to the top deck and called out to my accomplices who lay in wait in the dark shadowy undergrowth. They boarded the yacht, carrying between them a roughly constructed coffin. By now Jennifer's tongue had swollen to twice its size and she could no longer swallow, she could not feel herself breathing or sense her own pulse. Inside she was crying, sobbing her anguished heart out, but her eyes shed no tears, her pupils were dilated and her respiratory organs were non-functional. She was dead, or so it would seem! Jennifer, seeing the makeshift coffin, realised the fate that awaited her. She promised herself that in this life or the next she would reap her revenge on Miguel, her sadistic husband.

The lid of the coffin was opened and Jennifer's lifeless body was lowered into it. She watched in horror as the lid was slowly lowered. But suddenly its descent was halted. Thank God, she thought, I have been reprieved, but the descent of the lid was only halted so that a big black hand could insert a parting gift. Jennifer could see the long black hairy leg of a tarantula protruding between the fingers of her black assassin's hand. She felt the thud of the gigantic spider as it landed next to her face as the coffin lid was screwed down fast. She tried to scream but nothing came out. They carried the coffin out to a waiting van so they could transport her to her final resting place in the dead of night. After about half an hour of driving over bumpy, unmade roads they came to the secret graveyard, used by Satanists for satanic ritual murders, where many a missing Haitian lay undiscovered. The devil-worshipping priest and priestesses were there to attend to the burial and so were a host of followers who were high on some kind of illusionary drug; then every ritual debauchery and blasphemy ensued. Jennifer could hear the chants as she felt the coffin being lowered into the cold ground. She felt the first shovelful of earth land on the coffin lid with a thud, then another and another, until the chanting and laughter became muffled and subdued. She could hear the exultant screams of pleasure as copulating couples frolicked in a frenzy upon the sacred ground above her. Whilst Jennifer's life lay suspended in limbo, I indulged myself in bizarre sexual acts, grinding my loins into the young-ebony bodied nymph who craved my seed with an insatiable satanic lust. "Take that, you bitch," I screamed as my loins jerked and sent a shudder of delight through the ebony nymph seductress whom I had just inseminated with my seed. But my words were not meant for my lustful partner, whom I had rode like a Gaucho breaking in a young mare, my grimy fingernails like spurs gouging her bare buttocks raw, but for Jennifer's ears.

As I now disentangled myself from the clutches of the daughter of Satan, a group of wailing impassioned followers of the silken, ebony-bodied high priestess stood in line, their simmering passion boiling over, as they gratefully took their turn to impregnate the sorceress with their rampant seeds, each hoping theirs would be fertilised as the black magic powers of her majesty would be passed on to her offspring. Jennifer lay motionless, entombed in her doomed pit of hell, praying for salvation and revenge.

I awoke in a cold sweat, knowing I would never be free of my demons or indeed of the voodoo that even now, like an invisible magnetic force, drew me back to Haiti; it was a force that I was powerless to resist. Haiti has long been the epicentre of the religion known as Voodoo. The word voodoo derives from the word 'Vodu' in the Fon language, which means 'Spirit God'. Voodoo is a religion. The distillation of profound religious ideas that originated in Africa during the slave trade era. It is a fusion of a number of religious traditions of which Catholicism is just one influence. Haitian culture and religions were formulated and inspired by virtually all of Africa, from Senegal to Mozambique. Voodoo is based on a dynamic relationship between the living and the spirit realm. The living give birth to the dead, the dead become the spirit and the spirits are the multiple expressions of the divine.

There were extreme elements that used the religion to further their own satanic and dark devil worship and they hijacked the voodoo religion to propagate their own depraved interpretation that soured the reputation of the voodoo religion.

11

SUSAN

Miguel had hoped to convince us to extend our time together so he could introduce us to the delights that awaited on his planned island-hopping trip to St. Lucia, Antigua and St. Martin. However, Silver Mist had now been blown far out into the Caribbean Sea and he had no idea of our current position, so he would have to study the charts and take compass bearings. The violent storm that had battered us for so long had, at last, abated and the clear blue sky was awash with chattering gulls, whose boisterous shrieks had awoken the others. The sea was like a tranquil blue milk pond with an eerie stillness that becalmed Silver Mist. Andrea was the first to speak.

"Thank God we are all right. I am glad that the storm is over and that has got to be one of the worst nights of my life."

"Yes," I agreed, "it was hell. Do you guys have any idea where we are," I asked.

Roman turned to Miguel. "Well, Captain, where do you think we are."

"I am not sure of our position but going by the compass and our last charted position I would say somewhere near Grenada," replied Miguel. Roman and Miguel descended below deck to see if they could get the engines going, after a short while the two men reappeared on deck. "I'm afraid it's useless, the salt water has got into the diesel tank and I have no spare fuel," said Miguel. "We'll have to wait for the wind to pick up and continue under sail power," explained Miguel. It was indeed an irony that the storm force winds that had tossed Silver Mist around in the swirling waters, like a cork in a cauldron, had now abandoned us to drift on the tide. At least the sun had appeared on the horizon and all looked well with the world. The warmth of the sun began to permeate our soggy clothes and a feeling of wellbeing engulfed our senses.

After a couple of hours drifting with the tide Roman sighted land. Sure enough we were drifting towards a small island. Miguel hurriedly dropped the anchor that entered the silken blue green waters with a splash. In the blink of an eye and in less than a heartbeat we were all four deposited in the rowing boat. Miguel and Roman pulling on the oars with all their might soon made land fall. Miguel leapt out of the rowing boat and grabbed a rope and beached the craft. Roman steadied the craft and allowed Andrea and I to disembark gracefully, like the ladies we undoubtedly were. Soon we were lying flat out on the warm, white, shimmering sand. As we relaxed we found ourselves gazing wondrously upon deep green vegetation and tall slender palm trees swaying gently in the warm tropical breeze; the breeze was scented with the fragrance of tropical wild flowers and rich dense vegetation. The scent of wild orchids hung in the air and colourful butterflies danced on the breeze, their wings all a flutter. The opal blue sky was clear with not a cloud in sight. The pure white sand glistened with a silver lustre as the sun's tentacles, like ingots of gold, gently bathed them in a warm radiant heat that dried our wet, dishevelled clothes and healed our exhausted bodies.

Roman and Andrea rose to their feet, leaving Miguel and I flat out on the beach. Hand in hand they wandered off into the undergrowth. Roman turned to look at Andrea, her flaxen gold hair glistened in the sunlight and her eyes were warm and compassionate, like tranquil pools of water, reflecting colours in perpetual motion. Her perfectly formed features were unsullied from the sun's arrogant glow. Every time he looked into Andrea's eyes his head seemed to swim like a turbulent whirlpool. She was as intoxicating as a rum punch on a clear moonlit night and her eyes sparkled with an iridescent glow like spangled moonlight. Andrea felt Roman's hot, passionate breath on her face as he took her in his embrace; she lifted her head and with her cool, blue, sequined eyes she looked deeply into his. Her soft, rose petal lips melted as they touched Roman's warm, wet, sensual mouth. She felt a volcanic eruption in the pit of her stomach that sent seismic tremors down to her toes. Andrea gently released herself from Roman's clasping arms. Turning her head to one side, she gave him a sultry, evocative, knowing smile that urged him to, once again, take her voluptuous curvaceous body into his arms as they sank to their knees in the clammy, wet sand, kissing passionately and feverishly, tearing at their dishevelled clothes. Andrea's exultant cries of delight were masked by the incoming crashing waves; Roman's Machiavellian disregard for all around him was driven by the overwhelming desire to copulate.

Following a period of recuperation Roman took Andrea's hand and led her towards the shade of a cluster of palm trees leaving Miguel and I making out on the beach. On the breeze we could smell the scent of pine forests and lemon groves. Andrea's hair had become knotted and tangled in the wind and their rumbustious love-making, so with consummate expertise and an air of vanity, she combed it with a pine cone that she had found languishing in the undergrowth. "That feels better," she said as she tossed her head from side to side, the movement of her hair in an arc around her shoulders. "Go and see if Susan and Miguel have finished messing about, I want to explore the island," instructed Andrea. Roman wandered off and as requested returned with Miguel and I in tow. We headed into the thick, strangely forbidding undergrowth. As we carved a passage through the dense thicket, it became obvious that the island was uninhabited. We felt like early explorers entering into nature's inner sanctum, a tinge of excitement pulsating through our veins. For all our exultant excitement there remained a sinister feeling of foreboding. The absence of man's footprint on the island was evident: no cars or radios to disturb the peace and tranquillity of this beautiful cornucopia, only the weird animated sounds of the jungle could be heard. Bird song soaring into infinity; the chitter chatter of animals screeching and scurrying through the greenery before us.

We two couples, hands clasped together, were ourselves strangely muted, our eyes and senses drinking in all that was around us. It was all we could do to remember to breathe such was the intensity of beguilement. Suddenly we stumbled upon a clearing that had, at some point, been made by man and just beyond, which lay undisturbed for decades, was the remnants of the lemon grove that we had smelt on the breeze earlier. The deserted, one-time plantation was overgrown and unattended for years, it seemed. As we continued our trek ever inward towards the epicentre of the island, we became more and more enchanted with this tiny tropical paradise, a metaphoric Shangrila. We came upon a multitude of mango trees, their branches over loaded with ripe mangoes that applied with the early morning dew, shone with a gleaming lustre in the sumptuous warm tropical sunlight. There were a number of breadfruit trees as well as banana and wild cherry trees. Cascading cherry blossom lay in an array of pink haze all around us, about our heads their fluttered leaves of green, yellow and scarlet that were like confetti before a blushing bride. The coconut trees that populated the coastline were conspicuous in their absence amongst the abundant undergrowth greenery. The various shades of green surrounding us contrasted well with lovely pinks, blues, reds, purples and oranges of the tropical flowers that lay at our feet, like a multi coloured carpet, covering the jungle floor.

The strong lingering scents were a cacophony of smells that filled the lungs and captivated the senses, and paled into insignificance the best efforts of Coco Chanel.

Gazing upon nature's bounty only served to remind us that we had not eaten and were, indeed, feeling the pangs of hunger. Miguel climbed a yam tree, its branches heaving with ripe fruit, and Roman climbed up a banana tree tossing a huge hand of bananas to me, while Miguel handed down some juicy ripe yams to Andrea. From his elevated position at the top of the tree Miguel could see the reflection of water somewhere in the distance. "Can you see what I can see?" enquired Miguel. "There seems to be a lake or something in the distance, I can see the sun glinting off the surface."

"Yes I can see it too," replied Roman. "Hopefully it's not a mirage; we could do with some fresh water to drink and it would be lovely to take a swim in a nice cool lake." Miguel and Roman descended from their trees and enjoyed the fruits of their labour, along with myself and Andrea. We tucked into the fruits of the forest and ate our fill, the succulent bounty would sustain us for now.

We decided it was now time to continue our journey ever deeper into the island's interior in search of the lake that Miguel and Roman had seen from the top of the trees. By now, the four of us were all suffering from the intense heat and were sweating, the salt from the sea water stinging as we perspired. It would, indeed, be good to immerse our tired, aching bodies in the cool waters of the lake, but we had to locate it first. Seeing the lake from the tree tops was one thing, finding it ploughing through the wooded undergrowth of the interior was another matter entirely. As we continued our quest Andrea screamed out in pain as some insect stung her at the top of her thigh. We looked up to see swarms of insects of biblical proportions closing in on us. We dived headlong into the undergrowth to avoid the pursuing antagonists, as the army of insects disappeared into the distance we emerged unharmed but dishevelled. The intensity of the sun's golden rays imparted such intense heat that it almost scythed us down – like being struck with a red hot sabre. It could not be endured much longer; we had to find shelter and that elusive tantalising lake. We needed fresh water to drink as our throats felt like we had swallowed a prickly pear.

It seemed that we had been walking for hours when, at last, we came upon a beautiful lake nestled in amongst the pine forest, the sun's rays dancing off its cool effervescent indigo waters. The lake was fed by a meandering stream that descended from a rocky crag, forming a waterfall that created a bubbling, swirling cauldron below. The air we inhaled was damp from the spray that covered all the colourful vegetation and flowering shrubs in a fine layer of moisture that glistened and shone in the bright unforgiving sun. It was reminiscent of a picture-perfect postcard scene, totally unspoilt and bathed in sumptuous, warm, tropical sunlight that seemed to gently lick the plant's petals with a dark red glow, like a faithful dog licking his master's hand. The branches of the numerous trees that surrounded the lake hung limply in its tranquil waters of indigo deep and wide. Andrea and I were the first to make our way down to the water's edge and soon found ourselves gazing hypnotically into the mysterious, yet enchanting, depths of the silky alluring water.

I was the first to strip off as I plunged headlong

into the water. Andrea, not to be outdone, tore off her ragged clothes and dived in next to me.

"Shit, it's freezing," I gasped. The shock of the cold took Andrea's breath away as she spluttered a reply that was consequently inaudible. Miguel and Roman soon discarded their clothes and were playfully frolicking about in the icy blue waters with Andrea and I. The deep clear water engulfed us with a serene embrace that gently bathed away the pain of our weary sun-scorched bodies. Miguel watched intently as I swam beneath him, my lovely curvaceous sensual body cutting a swathe through the nerve tingling icy waters. For a while we played and fondled our partners in gay abandon as we fell under the spell of the enchanting island, but we had to get out of the icy water before we lost all feeling. We eventually dragged ourselves from the water and laid outstretched at the water's edge lazily drying off under the warm tropical sun that had, by now, lost some of its intensity.

Andrea and I laid on our backs peering skyward, our fulsome breasts standing to attention, like soldiers on parade, the cold water making our nipples stiff and erect. It was a sight not lost on Miguel and Roman. I sat up and pulled my skimpy top over my head, my breasts still wet. My white top became transparent as it clung to my pert, wet young breasts, even the goose pimples that had resulted from the shock of the icy-cold water was clear to see. I stood up in front of Miguel and slowly but purposefully pulled up my short, tight skirt, affording him a long, lingering glimpse of my magnificent pubic forest. Somehow seeing me naked was nowhere near as

83

exciting as watching me dress, Miguel felt embarrassed by the subsequent movement in his trousers. He was sure I had noticed. Andrea meanwhile demurely put her clothes on behind a clump of foliage, not treating Roman to the same erotic display.

If we were going to explore the island any further that day, we would have to make haste whilst there was still plenty of day light left. We decided to carry on exploring the island, going further and further away from the safety of Silver Mist. Every now and again spangled rays of sunlight broke through the dense canopy above, darting jets of gold gently touching the forest floor and bathing the fauna in a warm glow that sustained and nurtured life. It was imperative that we did not stray too far as it was amazing how quickly day turned to dusk and dusk to night, in an encompassing blackness that would engulf us. It would be all but impossible to find our way back in the black shroud of nightfall.

Suddenly we emerged from the forest's canopy to find ourselves gazing upon a hilly outcrop that rose up into the fluffy white clouds that hovered in the opal blue sky above. We climbed a rocky path and eventually found ourselves at the apex of the mound, this was the highest point on the island and made a perfect vantage point to survey all that was around us. We could now see the rugged shoreline on the opposite side of the island, it looked deserted and strangely unreal, almost as if the whole scene had been contrived for our benefit. We could see for the first time how far we had ventured. Silver Mist's mast could only just be seen out in the lagoon. It was time we started making our way back before the sun withdrew from the sky. Having just made it back to the rowing boat in time, as the darkness descended with Miguel and Roman pulling feverishly at the oars, it was not long before we were safely deposited on board Silver Mist once more.

Andrea and I raided the supplies to cook a light supper before retiring for the night. I said goodnight to Roman, squeezing past him, making sure my protruding nipples grazed his cheek as my skimpy top revealed my ample milk-white bosom. Grabbing Miguel's hand I looked sheepishly into Miguel's eyes. "Come on, darling, I feel like an early night." I smiled ruefully. Andrea and Roman were left alone, staring into each other's eyes. Roman felt very uncomfortable when I flirted with him, especially in front of Andrea. "I don't fancy Susan," exclaimed Roman going on the defensive. "I don't know why she is always coming on to me." Andrea grabbed the zip on Roman's trousers. "For someone who doesn't fancy Susan," exclaimed Andrea "the bulge in your trousers suggests otherwise." Andrea smiled serenely. "Don't worry about it, Roman, she's always been the same, it's just the way she is. I'm used to it by now, her trouble is that she thinks every man wants her and, of course, most do. Come on let's have a stroll around the deck before we go to bed," suggested Andrea. Arm in arm they walked around the small deck taking in the wonderful warm night air filled with the scent of wild flowers and mixed with the salty sea spray. Andrea held Roman's hand tightly as she stared wistfully up into the night sky. The map of the moon reflecting on her beautiful face, beneath her feet lay the shadowy depths of the Caribbean Sea and above her head the sea of tranquillity. As she peered up at the stars, Andrea fancied she could see lunar dust strewn across the heavens.

Andrea turned her attention to Roman, her eyes like falling lilac blossom, fell upon her lover under a blanket of stars that shone almost as brightly as her love for Roman. Roman could see the warm comforting glow of love in Andrea's eyes and by the feeling of exhilaration that pulsated through his veins whenever she was in his arms he knew he felt the same. They were kindred spirits destined to remain entwined in each other's arms for eternity. Andrea was like a celestial angel that fell to earth to land at his feet in an array of cherry blossom that floats on temperate breeze. Hand in hand Roman and Andrea returned to their cabin to consummate further their love for one another and to, eventually, fall into a blissful night's sleep enraptured in each other's arms.

12

Roman awoke in the morning to the sound of frantic love-making in our cabin next door. He laid motionless whilst Miguel and I copulated noisily in our bunks, whilst my screams of exultation urged Miguel to an earth-quaking climax. Andrea awoke and coyly looked at Roman, a broad grin spread across her face. Roman leaned over and kissed Andrea's rose-petal lips. After a few seconds of silence they heard me get up and wander out to the bathroom; on the way back I rapped my knuckles on Roman's door. "Are you getting up?" I enquired. "We're having breakfast soon, perhaps you could row me ashore, Roman, and help me collect some fresh fruit from the island," I added. Roman had panic in his eyes. I think he dreaded being isolated on the island with me. He knew that I was intent on having my way with him. Of course, what really bothered Roman was that he knew that he couldn't trust his own carnal urges and would surely succumb to my advances. My seductive powers rarely failed me. I would have my man and I would have him soon. I was concerned that Andrea, the poor love, was falling for Roman in a big way, I could see it in her dewy eyes every time she looked at him. I think it's a bit soon to be falling in love. Me, I'm just happy to have some fun. If love should come my way, so be it, but I'm not holding my breath. I want to see just how loyal Roman is when I get him alone on the island and offer my sex to him on a plate. Will he be able to control his primeval urges and keep his dick in his pants? Hmm, I wonder. By the time Roman had showered and dressed I was already on deck alongside Miguel, who was pouring over some navigational charts trying to determine our position after being blown off course in the ferocious storm.

Roman greeted Miguel and I. "Good morning, I hope you both slept well,"

"Good morning," replied Miguel. "I slept like a baby," he grinned.

I interrupted, "Yes but you woke up a bit stiff this morning, didn't you, my love? But I think I might have relieved you of that." I giggled and beckoned Roman to follow me. "Come on, Roman, let's get in the rowing boat and collect some fresh ripe fruit from the island to have with our breakfast." Roman climbed over the side and installed himself in the rowing boat, he then held out his hand and I clasped it tightly as I lowered myself into the boat. As Roman started to row for shore Miguel called out to him, "I would be careful if I were you, my friend, Susan has that look in her eye that suggests she is on the prowl." Miguel laughed and waved them off. Roman feared that his words would not turn out to be in jest.

As Roman pulled slavishly on the oars he looked at my pouting lips; I looked almost subdued and calm, perhaps it would be alright after all Roman pondered. He suddenly realised that he would be disappointed if I did not try anything after all. Roman had done his best to fend off my advances, most of the time, but it would not be his fault if I forced myself upon him, he could claim to be the victim of my lustful depravity. Roman ran the rowing boat aground with a thud that brought me into his arms, my hand coming to rest in his lap. "I am sorry about the jolt," exclaimed Roman.

"Oh that is all right." I retorted, "I'm still in one piece. More to the point, I've got you all to myself, alone at last." I smiled lustfully. "Don't you want to touch me too," I took Roman's hand and placed it between my legs. He could feel the warmth and wetness through my translucent white shorts that I had hurriedly put on after my shower. I wriggled my hips flirtatiously, forcing Roman's hand to rub my inner thigh. Something inside Roman snapped; he had to have me there and then! As our bodies locked together in a throbbing embrace we rolled over the side of the boat and into the shallow water still rolling over and over until we came to rest on the shimmering white beach. By now we were both naked and fully aroused, the soft white sand had become embedded in the crevices of our wet smouldering bodies. This was pure unadulterated lust! Roman knew that I had not long come from a rendezvous between the sheets with Miguel, as he had woken to our lustful cries of pleasure aboard Silver Mist, and now I was with him still drenched in the passion of love's seed, my portal overflowing. I sank my teeth into Roman's neck and plunged my tigress-like talons into his arched back.

My insatiable lust for carnal pleasure boiled over. As we kissed passionately, mine and Roman's tongues exploded on contact, like two meteors colliding in space. Roman's mouth was all over my milky-white flesh, his tongue exploring the inner sanctum of my voluptuous body, my taste as sweet as strawberries and cream on a sultry summer's day. My ample breasts bounced up and down and from side to side as Roman's whole body went into erotic spasms. I screamed encouragement in Roman's ear and my body, too, shuddered as Roman neared the end of his long journey into the deep humid jungle's interior erogenous zone.

Like a spent firework Roman fizzled to a halt, he rolled over onto his back exhausted. He lay motionless and subdued his mind in turmoil as his heart was racked with guilt, like most men he had been unable to control his animal urges and now was the time for self-recriminations. Roman had betrayed the woman that he had professed to love for a few fleeting moments of biological madness and now I would have a hold over him. He feared he would be at my beck and call whenever the mood took me. I was bound to drop little hints and innuendos in front of Andrea, he thought. That would be half the fun to me to suggest impropriety between myself and Roman, to subtly let her know that I had had my lustful way with her man. Roman rose to his feet glancing down at me almost contemptuously and suggested we had better collect the fruit we had come for. Roman walked towards the lemon groves, his head hung low, weighted down by the tortuous knowledge of his infidelity. I on the other hand sprang to my feet with boundless joy and gleefully ran after Roman, as I caught up with him, I clasped my hand in his. "What's up Roman?" I quipped sarcastically. "Feeling a bit guilty now, are we?" I giggled. "Okay come on, lighten up, it was only a bit of fun". Roman stoically said nothing, keeping his own council. Roman tugged his hand from my clasp with disdain. He strode on ahead, more angry with himself than with me, after all I could not help myself, I saw nothing wrong in what we had done. I had an insatiable lust for sex that just had to be satisfied, like a raging thirst that had to be quenched.

By now I was running to keep up with him. I grabbed hold of his arm and forced him to stop walking. "Okay I'm sorry I tricked you into making love to me, but be honest with yourself, you were as eager as I was," I exclaimed. Roman shook his head and muttered to himself, self-denigration no doubt. "Come on, what's done is done we can't change what has happened." I smiled. "Don't worry" I went on "I'll not tell Andrea, why would I? She would hate me too." I squeezed his arm tightly and smiled reassuringly. For the first time Roman felt he could trust me, he had an innate feeling that I would not let him down. It was now just a matter of whether he could conceal his own guilt and remorse from Andrea. He knew he had to bury his guilt if he and Andrea were going to spend the rest of their lives together.

Meanwhile Andrea was stood on the deck looking out anxiously towards the island, fearing the worst. She did not trust me to be alone with Roman all this time. Of course she trusted Roman, but she knew my seductive charms were hard to resist. Suddenly the rowing boat came into view with Roman pulling hard on the oars, I smiled serenely, my clothes somewhat dishevelled. The boat was heaving with its heavily laden load of ripe fruit. As we drew alongside Roman tossed the rope to Miguel so he could secure the boat to the yacht. Once we had clambered back on board and unloaded our spoils we sat around chatting and devouring breakfast. I, as I had promised, made no reference to the sexual explosion that had taken place between me and Roman on the island. There was something incredibly erotic about knowing I had Roman in every conceivable position behind my friend's back. Just having that knowledge was like a narcotic buzz.

Miguel had not been sitting idle whilst we were gathering fruit on the island, he had been busy plotting our course for the nearest inhabitable island, having established our current position. The winds had got up, enabling our party to set sail and to leave behind us, in our wake, the tiny tropical paradise island with its lush fauna and sumptuous fruits on which we had gorged ourselves. A fresh gust of wind blew out the crumpled canvas with a resounding clap and soon Silver Mist sped over the shimmering aquamarine waters with renewed vigour. Miguel had plotted a course for St. Lucia, it being the nearest inhabited island. As enchanting as the small tropical island was it would be good to get back to civilisation and to escape the somewhat bijou confines of the yacht's cabins for a more sumptuous hotel room with a bath, soft clean towels and a change of clothes, maybe a chance to dress up and enjoy a night out somewhere posh and sophisticated, really expensive. Well Roman and Miguel could afford it, I thought to myself.

13

As we approached St. Lucia the outstretched palms seem to beckon to us with a welcoming wave. Miguel released the anchor and the splash as it entered the pearly warm water showered us with cascading droplets that tingled our skin. Once more in the bustling bay we found ourselves transported into a world of Caribbean magic. With tropical rainforests covering its distinctive mountain called the Pitons and its beguiling beaches lining its shores St. Lucia was unlike any other Caribbean Island. We disembarked Silver Mist and climbed into the dinghy, rowing easily, the gentle swish of the oars as we carved our way through the calm waters of the picturesque bay. On the breeze we could smell the unmistakeable fragrance of Jasmine that were intertwined with nutmeg and tamarind trees deep in the forest. Our lungs were full with exotic smells and our heads dizzy with exhilaration. We landed ashore, once we had disembarked onto dry land we made our way to the nearest hotel. We found a rather fetching Boutique Hotel, the foyer decked in stunning white marble and huge swirling fans hung from the decorative gold leaf ceiling adding a welcome chill to the air. The cool breeze from the fans made my nipples even more prominent in my skimpy low-cut top, which did not go unnoticed by the concierge standing behind the front desk.

After we had signed the register we dumped what little luggage we had and went in search of the nearest bar. I, especially, was looking forward to a long cool glass of Caribbean rum punch festooned with zesty fruits and babbling ice cubes. Andrea had a non-alcoholic cocktail; the sun always gave her a headache if she drank too much in the day. Miguel and Roman clasped their fingers around a large cool beer. After a short while Miguel and I slinked off to find our room and to freshen up before exploring the local market place and the tourist traps. Andrea and Roman found their room and had a cool refreshing shower together before setting off to meet Miguel and me at a pre-arranged rendezvous in the market square. It was mid-afternoon and the scorching sun's golden rays cascaded through the branches of the trees that overhung the market square, giving some shade. Andrea and I wandered off together in search of a designer outlet where we could find something suitably expensive to spend Miguel and Roman's money on. We were eager to find something seductive that would bring out the primitive in Roman and Miguel. As evening drew near we met up with Miguel and Roman and went back to our rooms to change.

Andrea and I dressed up as seductively as we dare, having applied our make up with consummate precision; a bit of blusher here and just a hint of lip gloss there. Andrea was not brave enough to wear such a revealing and plunging neckline as me, but she felt sexy all the same and she hoped Roman would appreciate the effort she had made to look her best. Miguel and Roman waited for what seemed like hours, for us to ready ourselves for the night ahead, they were not disappointed when we eventually made an entrance. I stood in a provocative pose in my slinky, black, sequined evening gown with its plunging neckline that almost exposed my belly button, my fulsome breasts barely contained. The dress was backless so I could not wear a bra, so hoped gravity and a bit of double-sided tape would spare my blushes. Andrea, meanwhile, stood nervously in my shadow her brightly coloured silk dress, like water colours running in the rain, clung to her young body like a second skin. We walked into the hotel's pulsating dance hall, I clutching my glitzy clutch bag and wearing my Jimmy Choo shoes, with heels so high, as to make me appear unsteady on my feet. Our ears were pounding from the thumping beat from the enormous speakers in the corner. The D.J. manipulated his strobe lighting to shine directly at Andrea and myself, to the delight of the men there, showing our womanly charms to the full.

I took centre stage, my tight white panties clung to my curvaceous buttocks. I whisked my way towards a group of bronzed young Adonises, their tight jeans and t-shirts bulging under their rippling muscles. I could smell the testosterone burning my nostrils. Miguel looked on helplessly as I cavorted and gyrated in between the handsome young studs. He could sense I was becoming more and more aroused, the strobe lighting exposing my erect nipples. Meanwhile Roman and Andrea were clinging to each other as more people crammed onto the dance floor. Miguel had seen enough and decided it was time to drag me out of there. He snatched my hand forcibly, dragging me off the dance floor.

"What the hell are you doing?" I raged. "I was just having a good time."

"Perhaps you might like to have a nice time with me," Miguel suggested. "After all I bought that damn dress that you're flirting in." I realised I had gone too far and was in danger of losing my rich suitor. "I'm sorry, my darling, I didn't mean to upset you. I will make it up to you later," I begged for forgiveness. As Miguel stared into my eyes, transfixed, all he could think of was how he was going to persuade me to travel with him and Roman to Haiti. Miguel felt an irresistible urge to return to Haiti, as if something was pulling him back there. The demons that infiltrated Miguel's mind began to summon up dark thoughts of the kind of despair that had led to his wife's ultimate demise. Little did I know but my fate hung in the balance of a mind unbalanced.

Miguel and Roman were growing tired of the noise and frenetic mayhem of the dance hall and persuaded Andrea and I to accompany them on a moonlight stroll. Soon we found ourselves walking along the beach, the white sand reflecting beams of moonlight. Andrea and I removed our designer shoes and allowed the incoming waves to wash over our feet that were sore from dancing. As we looked out into the bay we could just make out Silver Mist's white sails silhouetted against the black Caribbean night sky. There appeared to be a beach party on the other side of the bay, we could hear music and laughter and the blackness of the night sky was punctuated by bright exploding fireworks that lit up the horizon. The fireworks created a blaze of colour that filled the sky and a cacophony of sounds that assaulted our ears. "Why don't we go and get the dinghy and row back out to the yacht?" suggested Miguel. "We'll be able to see the fireworks better from there." We all agreed it was a good idea, in fact, we decided that it would be far too hot to go back to the stuffy hotel room for the night. It would be far more pleasant sleeping under the stars on Silver Mist's deck.

Once back on the yacht we watched the remainder of the fireworks display and could make out the revellers' voices in the distance over the surging waves that slapped against the bows of the yacht. Rockets screamed across the black velvet Caribbean sky freefalling into the swirling abyss of the sea, spent, their life extinguished. As the debris of the last rocket hurled to earth and the display came to an end an eerie silence ensued only broken by the crashing of the waves against Silver Mist's hull. Miguel and I decided to sleep in our bunks below deck after all and said our goodnights to Roman and Andrea, who remained on deck. Roman looked down at Andrea, her sculptured form captured under the scattered light that trickled from the fleeting moon, Andrea's colourful translucent wet gown clung to her body and exposed her nakedness under the jewelled moonlight. Roman became the victim once more of the rising tide of emotion that swelled up inside him like the magma throbbing inside a volcano, waiting to erupt. The urge to lift up Andrea's gown and to bury his face in her lovely soft warm love spot became too great to resist. Her sweet taste like ambrosia to the gods of Mount Olympus. Andrea groaned with delight, like a cat purring with satisfaction as it consumes the cream. Andrea found herself unceremoniously pushed up hard against the yacht's mast, her legs spread wide apart, yearning for the mainsail to be hoisted. Roman was only too happy to oblige and as he steered his rudder into port the ecstasy of dropping anchor released a flood of love seeds that surged forth unabated. The mast creaked and groaned under the strain and the haunting wind whistled through the rigging to the sound of loves refrain.

Like a loyal subject Roman knelt before his goddess kissing her feet and sucking her toes erotically. Andrea was in seventh heaven and was totally consumed in a warm glow of utter satisfaction. She could not help but contemplate an exciting and fulfilled future with Roman at her side, as content and warm as the sun in the sky. Andrea dreamed of walking down the aisle in a flowing white gown and kneeling at the altar beside her handsome groom. The two lovers decided that they would, at last, have to concede to father time and let the night come to an end. They huddled together amongst some old sails and fell asleep, in each other's arms, under a star-spangled black velvet sky.

Down below deck I was having a lurid dream about my teenage years back in England. I had, over those years, many assignations with young men in the local graveyard where I lived. I spent many memorable evenings climbing the steep steps up to the Abbey that was perched, like a pinnacle, on top of the hill. It proved to be an ideal place to rendezvous with my adolescent lovers, no one ever disturbed us. There was something incredibly erotic about being seduced in a graveyard, being plundered from behind, whilst bent over a cold damp gravestone. I had a devilish disregard for the sanctity of sacred ground and revelled in delight at the thought of those disapproving corpses that lay dormant in their coffins below. I had always found true love elusive and was, anyway, unwilling to commit to a steady relationship and considered monogamy boring. However, I now felt that I and Miguel could soon become inseparable, something I had not felt before. I could sense the seeds of love germinating and had realistic hopes of it blossoming into a fully-fledged romance. True I still found it difficult not to flirt with other men, but I was beginning to dread the thought of life without Miguel as it would leave an empty void that would be difficult to fill.

14

As I awoke from my dream I could hear Silver Mist's decks creaking as she rolled gently on the rippling tide. I fancied that I could also hear a low recurrent groaning sound that seemed to emanate from a third cabin that was always kept locked. When I had asked Miguel what was in the cabin he just told me that it was full of nautical equipment and junk that he had accumulated over the years. It was probably the sound of the wind howling through the rigging that I could hear, I told myself reassuringly. Every now and then my nose would twitch as I smelt a scented fragrance wafting into my cabin; it was there one minute and then next it would fade away making me wonder if I had imagined that too. I had a very sensitive nose when it came to perfumes, as I had once worked behind a cosmetics counter in Boots. The scent was not one of mine or Andrea's. It was very refined and probably very expensive, and just as I was about to put a name to it the smell would melt away and fade into the ether, leaving me to ponder on its origin. Sometimes it would hang in the air so thick that I could taste it. These mysterious sounds and smells, in the night aboard a yacht, upon the open sea intrigued me and inspired my sense of adventure. Soon it would be morning and the mysteries of the night would be forgotten.

Miguel had set the autopilot on course for St. Martins, but, mysteriously the setting had changed all by itself and we were now heading straight for Haiti. It was as if some strange force was at work, pulling Silver Mist ever closer to Haiti. Something or someone was summoning us back to the island of dark satanic voodoo spirits and the mystique of legend. As dawn became morning we had a refreshing shower and ate a hearty breakfast and then with a sense of resignation in his voice Miguel informed everyone that they had drifted so far off course that their intended destination, St. Martin, was not practical and we would have to journey on to Haiti. It was time to succumb to the dark forces of the underworld and accept our destiny. We would be entering the waters surrounding the voodoo island before the day was over. The prospect of entering the chilling twilight zone of Haiti under the shadowy cover of darkness filled Miguel's pulsating body with dread. He knew that he was powerless to resist the overwhelming satanic forces that lurked in the shadows. I could sense the foreboding in Miguel's voice and I could see the terror in his eyes. This induced a tension in all of us, without knowing why. We had intended to go to Haiti after St. Martin anyway, so why the foreboding now!

As Silver Mist eventually entered the swirling waters about a mile off Haiti a comforting calmness came over us. Miguel dropped anchor, the splash as it entered the water, breaking the deathly silence. Silver Mist rolled from side to side in the turbulent waters, her bows creaking, her rigging singing in the breeze. Andrea and I went below deck to prepare some supper, which we duly consumed and washed down with the usual amount of alcohol.

It was Miguel's intention all along to get us to Haiti, but part of him fought against the urge because he knew he may not be able to prevent something sinister happening once we and he were in the grip of black magic. Miguel took hold of my hand and steered me away from Andrea and Roman, he put his arms lovingly around me as we leaned over the rail looking down into the deep abyss of the ocean. "Will you marry me, Susan?" Miguel asked. "I do love you and I think we would be good together." I was stunned for a moment and could not answer as Miguel's proposal had literally taken my breath away. I gulped in some air and swallowed nervously. "Yes, yes of course I'll marry you," I stuttered. I screamed in elation which attracted the attention of Roman and Andrea. "What's all the commotion and excitement about," enquired Andrea. She knew her friend was prone to bouts of excitement, but this was incredibly spontaneous, even for me. "Miguel has asked me to marry him," I explained. "And I have accepted." I went on.

"This calls for a celebration," said Roman, "I'll go below and get the best bottle of bubbly that I can find." He emerged moments later with a suitably vintage bottle of champers and four tall stemmed glasses. We took a glass each and Roman poured the effervescent champagne till it overflowed. A toast was raised to the happy couple and all seemed serene and peaceful.

Although Andrea was pleased for me she still had a nagging doubt in her mind about Miguel and, indeed, whether I was ready to settle into domesticity and married bliss. It was good news for Andrea, maybe now Roman would be safe from my advances. Andrea felt that there was something strange about Miguel; he was charming enough, but below the surface there was a sense of internal struggle that he did his best to hide. He could appear opaque and superficial and was often preoccupied with something that clearly bothered him. Andrea could not put her finger on it but she felt that whatever it was that distracted Miguel was there in front of her, but she just could not see it. She always expected something to happen to confirm her suspicions but nothing ever did. Andrea was sure that one day, whatever he was hiding would surface and everyone would see but maybe then it would be too late or maybe she was just being irrational. It was time to get some sleep so they would be fresh in the morning to sail Silver Mist into Port-Au-Prince harbour. Miguel and I soon sank into a deep sleep, my head light from too much champagne.

Roman and Andrea were not as tired and as they cuddled up together Andrea nibbled Roman's ear and seductively poked her tongue in it whilst Roman ran his fingers through Andrea's fair silken hair. She was like a temptress egging him on encouraging him to touch her most private parts with his loving hands. Roman buried his face in Andrea's womanhood, the sublime fragrance of her young, eager body filled his lungs as he gulped for air, her scent as intoxicating as wild orchids bathed in early morning dew. Like an adolescent he worshipped her. He worshipped her with his mind, body and his soul. Roman was like a male peacock displaying his magnificent loins and his torso rippling with muscular power, like a medieval rampaging knight in gleaming armour, scaling the ramparts of a castle. Roman pulled down Andrea's drawbridge and crossed her moat entering her keep with his pulsating body rippling with muscular tension, perspiration running down his heaving chest, he was like an Adonis before her, acknowledging her admiration. Roman went into battle, his metaphorical musket loaded and primed ready to shoot. Andrea's defences were breeched and Roman, the conquistador, took his prize, penetrating Andrea's wanton body with each round that he fired. Roman explored every searing inch of quivering flesh. A seismic shockwave burst through Andrea's body, a million tingling nerve ends sizzled as she anticipated Roman's final assault. Roman's battle cry sent shivers down her back, like the charge of the Light Brigade, his army of seedlings sped forth hurtling towards certain oblivion. The battlefield lay strewn with the fallout of volcanic eruptions deep in Andrea's body. Roman's mouth made contact with Andrea's moist quivering rose-petal lips and as their tongues met they gorged themselves in mutual pleasure. Roman and Andrea lay exhausted next to each other and sank into a deep sleep.

No one heard the door of the spare cabin creak on its hinges or smelt the hypnotic aroma of the luxurious French perfume that emanated from the cabin and hung in the still air. In the next cabin Miguel and I were also in a deep sleep, but Miguel's troubled mind would not let him sleep peacefully, all his insecurities and anxieties manifested themselves in poetic form.

The shadow on the wall is a shadow in his mind

The shadows in his mind are the fears that he hides

The creaking stair, the illusion that someone is there

Holding his breath and staring into the dark secluded expansive abyss of the night, he waits.

Self-persecution and perpetual illusion throws his mind into total confusion.

A figure moves furtively across his room its hand moving slowly towards his bed pointing to an image upon the wall.

Birds of the night inhabit his privacy, the torsion tissue of their wings echo like thunder through the night.

Awesome winds release his inheritance of guilt and fright, the seclusion of his environment contacts and disintegrates out of sight.

Miguel was not the only one having dreams, I too was deep in a subconscious dream that melted away readily. My head was full of fantasies and my forthcoming wedding. Standing at the altar the blushing bride imagined that I was back in old Rome. Miguel, my centurion lover and protector, by my side, but, what was this? My lover disrobing me in the midst of an orgy to be admired by the preying eyes of the noble, ageing senators clad in their white togas. Me standing there like the goddess Venus awaiting to be consumed by the sex-hungry rampant hordes of old grey men of the senate and the centurion soldiers that swilled wine from golden goblets and lusted after my vivacious body. My toga slowly slipped from my shoulders to reveal my magnificent pert young breasts to the gasps and cheers of my audience. One tug and it was around my ankles leaving my body naked and ready to be invaded on all fronts. I found myself thrust onto a white marble slab, my legs forced apart, my shoulders pressed hard against the ice cold marble and as I stared up into cold remorseless eyes of my first invader all I could do was to capitulate in the face of such overwhelming odds.

"God bless Rome," I cried as the first centurion entered my pulsating, wet, heaving, clammy body. The second man, a second cousin of Caesar himself, cursed as he missed the target with the first thrust of his glistening weapon, but made up for it with vigour as he now rode me like a stallion on heat. The others were becoming impatient and Caesar's second cousin was forced to dismount his mare before depositing his seeds in my garden of Gethsemane. I roared like a lioness pitted against the gladiators in the arena. Snarling with contempt I hissed, scratched and mauled my assailants, but to no avail, the onslaught continued unabated, my young body violated and plundered like the very first orchard on earth; the forbidden fruits of Eden. The centurions were like serpents spewing out poisonous seeds that covered me from head to toe. A black slave surreptitiously peaking from behind a marble column watching, holding his breath in case he was discovered, as each man in turn tasted the delights of my flesh. This blushing bride deflowered before her wedding day.

Could this man I was about to marry really put me through such an ordeal just to satisfy his perversion, I wondered. I awoke in a cold sweat and in the light of day I wondered whether I was doing the right thing marrying Miguel. Perhaps allowing myself to be catapulted into a marriage after such a short acquaintance was foolhardy.

My mind was suddenly in turmoil, only a matter of days now and I would become the second Mrs. Valdez, unaware of the fate of the first. I soon realised it was just nerves getting to me and I was probably being irrational. As I turned on my side and put my arms around Miguel, I felt my whole body relax and with a deep sigh my fears ebbed away leaving me feeling rejuvenated and contented happy in the knowledge once more that I would soon be married. I closed my eyes and feeling reassured slid into unconsciousness. Suddenly, like falling through a black hole in space, I found myself standing at the altar for real, a euphoric Miguel at my side.

AT THE ALTAR

The loveliness of the blushing bride
Behind the veil she hides
Clad in her virginal white silken flowing gown of elegant
    grace
Her excitement hidden from prying eyes behind the veil
    her incarnate face
Her bronzed complexion glistening against her snow
    white gown
Rigid like a stone statuette she stands
Clasping the beauty in her hands
Her lips like the rose petals she held before her
Her hair floating in the warm tropical breeze, its fragrance
    sweet and rare
Her sequined eyes ablaze like the diamond on her slender
    finger

At the altar dare she linger
Her lovely hair coiled in ringlets dance to the pounding
of her heart
And the waves that crash upon the shore
Having said "I do" she and her love have become one and
must never part
Together along lives highways they will travel as one
And like the evergreens their love shall never die.

I felt the reassuring glow of warmth in my heart as the black Priest pronounced us husband and wife. Miguel slipped the sparkling gold band on my finger and the two of us embraced and kissed in front of the small congregation. Andrea, who had been my only bridesmaid, hugged me and Miguel and wished us happiness for the future. Roman shook Miguel's hand firmly squeezing his hand he looked deep into Miguel's eyes. "Look after her this time," Roman said pointedly. I looked ravishing in my low-cut silk and lace gown, its long train floating in the breeze. I glowed with the aura of someone in love. Down on the beach the festivities had begun, rum and Coke flowed freely, along with an abundance of punch which was adorned with ripe Caribbean fruits. A lavish feast awaited us.

Miguel suddenly froze, like a stone statue, as his eyes came to rest upon a shrouded morose figure, head bowed, lurking in the shadows in the shade of a swaying palm tree. He blinked so he could focus his eyes better against the blinding sun, but as quick as a heartbeat when he reopened them the mysterious figure had vanished leaving behind only a strong pungent fragrance that wafted towards him on the breeze. His whole body started to shake and convulse as he recognised the scent that filled the air he breathed; he could smell and taste her presence. For a fleeting moment Miguel thought he had seen a ghost, but surely it could not possibly be her. Could it? Miguel looked around feverishly to see if anyone had witnessed his disturbing reaction but felt assured that no one noticed his discomfort. He managed to regain some semblance of control over his quivering limbs but his confidence, it seems, was misplaced because the small gathering of villagers that he had arranged to attend his wedding ceremony were now standing still and staring at him in silence. Now the small gathering seemed to swell into a throng of onlookers that were strangely familiar.

As the sun began to sink below the Caribbean-blue horizon the sound of music and joyous celebrations filled the expanding air. All of a sudden the man who was leading the steel band walked up to me and, with a gleam in his eye, presented me with a single red rose and with the accompaniment of his band he began to sing to me in a rich velvety voice, that made me go weak at the knees. The tall six foot six inch Caribbean calypso singer eased into a romantic ballad that Miguel had written as a tribute to his lovely new bride.

THE FOUR WAYS OF LOVE

If east is east and west is west
Who do I love the best?

If south is south and north is north
The answer must be you of course
No other love had thrilled me like you do
With your dark brown hair and bright green eyes
No other could be lovelier than you
Like the wings of a fleeting dragonfly, my heart takes flight
I am the luckiest man in the world tonight
Thine sweet red lips of rose petals fair, your hair too
With so rare a hue
So when east is east and west is west
I know you love me the best
Upon your breasts my head will rest
As long as south is south and north is north
You will know I love you of course

Filled with emotion and tears forming in my eyes, I was deeply touched by the soulful voice and the sentiment contained within the song. As the sun disappeared below the horizon the darkness fell like a cloak over us and the sultry warm night air became still and menacing. I felt a sense of foreboding, as if something terrible was about to happen. Starting in a whisper, the crowd were now chanting something in Haitian, a cold fear griped Miguel's body as he recognised the words. I assumed the chanting, which had now intensified in volume, was some kind of ritual marriage ceremony that was giving thanks to god for the divine meeting of two souls, but I could not have been more wrong. Miguel understood the chanted words well enough and he knew in his heart that he only had a few precious hours of married bliss before THEY would come for me.

Miguel was acutely aware that he would be powerless to stop them. Memories of his first wife came flooding back, the way he had used the dark forces of voodoo to dispose of her was now about to claim his new wife for a ritual sacrifice to the devil. Why had he been so stupid to get embroiled in the occult.

15

Miguel took my petite hand in his and led me back towards Silver Mist. We could see the light from the lantern that hung from her mast, her rigging silhouetted against the black totality of night. Miguel decided that once on board Silver Mist he and I would consummate our marriage and he would make love to me as never before. This night might be the last time we lay together before he would have to deliver me into the clutches of the voodoo high priest, who would have his lovely young bride remarried, in a second ceremony, to become the bride of Satan. The chanting hordes of satanic disciples would feast and gorge themselves on my broken body. Miguel could hear the syncopated drumming in the distance and the familiar sound of chanting satanic voices on the breeze as his blood surged through his veins. Miguel wished he could just pull up the anchor and surreptitiously sail Silver Mist out of Port-Au-Prince under the cover of darkness but even the thought of escaping brought on a paralysing pain down his spine, as if someone had sunk a knife into him. I noticed the grimace of pain on Miguel's face.

"Are you all right, my darling, you are not ill are

you?" I enquired nervously. "No I'm fine," came the reply. "It's just the thought of losing you that pains me, like a dagger through my heart." Miguel lifted his head and stared, through tear sodden eyes; I could feel the anguish that pulsed through Miguel's veins but did not understand why he was so troubled. If only I knew what lay ahead and my impending fate. "Don't worry, my love, I shall never leave you, not ever." I snuggled up to Miguel, "You'll see we'll grow old together," I said poignantly. "We'll live in a little cottage with roses round the door and a garden filled with wild flowers". This made Miguel's heart sink further.

I began to disrobe, hanging my wedding dress and veil carefully above our bunk. As Miguel's eyes rested upon my breasts and curvy young body the animal passion running through his veins exploded. I groaned with pleasure as Miguel thrust his loins against mine, I sank my nails in his buttocks as he pounded me relentlessly. I could feel his hot breath on my face as his whole body shuddered with convulsions at the point of climax. Miguel rolled off, his body limp and exhausted. Meanwhile back at the wedding ceremony the festivities continued as the villagers ate, drank and made merry long after we newlyweds had vanished into the ebony night.

Andrea and Roman had wandered off on their own, giving Miguel and I time to ourselves aboard Silver Mist. They wandered off arm in arm into the thick wooded hillside well away from the sandy beach, stumbling upon a well-used pathway, they decided to follow it to see where it led. Although it was now dark they could see their way using Roman's flashlight and came upon giant moths and other strange flying insects circling ahead of them. Andrea felt the downdraft from the beating wings of a giant moth as it buzzed around her head, making a whirring sound that startled her. Just as they were contemplating turning back they heard some strange noises coming from deep in the undergrowth up ahead. Roman decided to investigate but Andrea was more reticent, fearing there may be danger ahead.

As Roman turned the next corner he found himself amidst a dense thicket and peering through the undergrowth he could hardly believe his eyes. He quickly extinguished his torch and in a hushed voice told Andrea to be very quiet. There in the clearing, exposed under a beam of moonlight, were dozens of strangely dressed people who were dancing and chanting the same words over and over again. Roman did not know what they were saying but he knew enough to realise that they had stumbled on some kind of ritual devil worship. Roman was reminded of the Spanish Inquisition when heretics were put on trial and if found guilty, as they generally were, they would be put to death in the most gruesome fashion. Roman knew that their best hope of salvation was to melt away silently into the safe cloak of darkness, for should they be discovered the consequences could be dire indeed. They contrived to watch from a safe distance and were horrified at what they witnessed.

A pretty young Haitian girl, no more than fifteen or sixteen years old, was being dragged by her hair into the centre of the crowd that had formed a circle and were still chanting loudly. Her clothes were ripped feverishly and unceremoniously from her young virginal body and the poor hapless girl stood there, naked and trembling with fear. Petrified she braced herself as the first man tried to penetrate her supple young body then one after another they viciously and mercilessly gang raped her, leaving her bleeding and sobbing uncontrollably. All the while other women looked on. It was hard for Roman and Andrea not to give out a shriek of disbelief. The girl was understandably hysterical by now, the air they inhaled was filled with the smell of sex and blood as the girl was used again and again for the sick perverted pleasure of her attackers. Eventually the poor girl collapsed to the ground unconscious, she could take no more humiliation and pain.

Andrea could hardly contain her revulsion and as she was about to scream out Roman put his hand over her mouth and gradually led her away to a place of safety, both of them trembling with fear. Andrea felt sick to the pit of her stomach, she wanted to throw up. Roman had to get Andrea away from this den of iniquity before they could be discovered. He shuddered to think of what fate would befall Andrea if the sex-crazed mob got their ghoulish hands on her. As they discreetly walked away Roman looked back over his shoulder, he could see men and women indulging in depraved sexual acts as others looked on and shouted obscene words of encouragement. It seemed of no consequence that a young girl had been brutally raped in front of them or that she now lay expiring at their feet. Life it seemed was cheap indeed. All of a sudden the high priest dismounted the whorish vixen that he was riding and brandishing a huge silver steel dagger lunged at the heart of the stricken teenager. Her life ebbed away before their eyes like a fleeting dragonfly whose life cycle is also too short. Her body jerked a few times before the life eventually drained from her disfigured face. After witnessing such primeval butchery and satanic depravity all Roman and Andrea wanted to do was to run forever, never stopping to look back. They decided not to report what they had seen as they did not know how far up the communal chain of authority these deviants had infiltrated.

Roman and Andrea feverishly made their way back to Silver Mist. Andrea ran breathlessly, perspiration running down the centre of her back, as her t-shirt, soaked in sweat, clung to her breasts bouncing uncontrollably as she ran. Her shorts were drenched in sweat and chafed the top of her legs the salt rubbing into her wounds. Cold perspiration, from fear, splattered her face as she tore her way through the undergrowth. They ran as fast as they could down to the shoreline and along the beach to where they had left the dinghy but, of course, the dinghy had gone. Susan and Miguel had already used it to row out to Silver Mist. Andrea and Roman had no choice but to swim out to the anchored yacht, its hull and mast just barely visible silhouetted against the stormy skyline. They had no idea of Miguel's involvement with the satanic voodoo powers of the underworld or his intention to lay to rest his second wife alongside his first, although Roman had his suspicions. As Andrea and Roman eventually hauled themselves aboard Silver Mist a deathly silence greeted them and the stench of decay mixed with an intoxicating pungent scent of extravagant

French perfume engulfed them. Andrea and Roman huddled together for a while for comfort. Looking back at the island it was difficult to believe what they had seen. Andrea could sense a presence lurking in the shadows and a chill ran down her spine.

Meanwhile, after Miguel had regained his strength, we continued to screw vigorously, oblivious to the danger that was about to engulf us. We were about to pay the ultimate price for our lust for each other. We never heard the cabin door open. We were too engrossed in sexual pleasure to notice a disturbed figure standing over us. I clasped my legs around Miguel's buttocks like a Trap Door Spider flinging its legs around its sullen prey. I plunged my long manicured nails, like a marauding tigress, into his back, while he was riding me like a stallion to victory. I screamed sexual obscenities in his ear: "Come on, you dirty bastard, give it to me." I screamed, my whole body pulsating with excitement. At this point I glanced up to see the raised hand that belonged to Jennifer, Miguel's first wife, holding aloft a gleaming razor-sharp steel blade. Her arm was raised, poised to strike, manic eyes flashing like beacons in the dark. The revenge of a tormented soul was about to be unleashed upon us.

She lunged at Miguel first with ferocious intent. The sickening thud as the blade plunged into his chest. The sound of metal against bone made me cringe. That same exotic perfume that had so often hung in the air and wafted into our cabins was now even heavier. Soon our assailant's blade would be turned on me. All this time, neither Miguel or I seemed to be able to scream or shout for help, as if paralysed by some hypnotic drug, my suspicions were that our champagne had been laced with some kind of narcotic, as I remember feeling a bit woozy afterwards. I could see the blade hovering above my head, but just couldn't do anything to avoid the vicious blows that rained down on me, as if in slow motion. I felt the agonising pain as the first few strikes scythed through my body, but as the onslaught continued the pain began to dull and I felt myself levitate on the cusp of death.

"For fuck sake, you mad bitch, you are going to take my life," I shouted but the words wouldn't come out. Why, why? I murmured to myself, what had I done to her! As my life seemed to be slipping away I glanced at Miguel and realised that he'd already gone.

Jennifer had given thanks, many times over, for the good samaritan who'd released her from her pit of hell, but now she had no quality of life: her legs were gangrenous and maggot-infested, and she was in constant pain. The only thing that had kept her going was the thought of revenge and to finally end her suffering. She now turned the bloodied blade on herself, snuffing out her own life, but as she drifted away she said, "Don't worry, my darling Miguel, I'm coming with you," not knowing that Miguel had already departed this world. She gasped her last breath as she too expired, leaving carnage in her wake.

I could hear Andrea and Roman laughing on deck and I heard Andrea's footsteps clattering down the ladder. As she opened our cabin door she gave out a penetrating scream that had Roman rushing to her side. Miguel and I were clasped together, naked and covered in blood that dripped onto the floor with the rhythm of a dripping tap.

My finger had been severed with its shiny new gold ring splattered with blood and sinew. My beautiful brilliant white wedding gown that was hung above our bed, was covered in blood and fragments of flesh and chippings of bone that emphasised the ferocity of the attack that had taken place. Roman, belatedly, tried to shield Andrea's eyes from the sight of our mutilated bodies. It was like a scene from a horror movie.

Andrea tried to scream again but this time nothing came out. She was frozen, petrified to the spot. Roman did his best to comfort her but he too was in shock. As Roman regained his senses he knelt by my side and, taking hold of my hand he felt my wrist for a pulse. After a few seconds he turned to Andrea. "I think Susan's gone, my love, I can't feel a pulse."

Shaking, Andrea put her hand over her mouth and gulped a breath of air as she started to sob. Roman could see from Miguel's injuries and wide open eyes that he was dead. I desperately wanted to let them know that I was still clinging to life but I was unable to move or speak, such was my paralysis. I could hear all that was being said.

Roman took Andrea's hand and led her up to the top deck. "I'll go and phone for the police," I heard him say. "I won't be long, I promise," Roman went on. Roman sat Andrea down and poured her a brandy before he left. "Sit there and don't move," Roman uttered as he left to get help. Andrea sat transfixed, traumatised by her ordeal. She did as Roman had insisted and didn't move from her spot. It seemed an age before Roman finally re-emerged. "I've called the police and ambulance but I think it's too late to save, Susan, I'm sure she's gone," Roman said, putting his arm around Andrea to comfort her. After a short while I could hear the distant sound of sirens as the police eventually arrived. I heard the gruff voice of a policeman quizzing Roman and Andrea about what had taken place, then the more dulcet tones of the plain-clothes detective asking more questions.

The detective left the uniformed officer to take statements from Roman and Andrea and came down below deck to see for himself the carnage and to secure the scene. He tutted to himself and shook his head. "What a shame, such a waste of a beautiful girl." Lieutenant Samuel Pirez muttered to himself as he looked directly at me. "Get the pathologist down here," he shouted.

As the pathologist entered the cabin he said, "I want you to confirm life extinct and time of death." Lieutenant Pirez made his way out of the cabin. The pathologist was not too thorough with his examination and quickly called for three body bags to be sent down, he also sent a message that the ambulance could leave as it would not be needed. At this point I really thought my time was up, no one could see I was still alive and all the time I could feel the blood haemorrhaging from my broken body, but somehow I still clung to life.

I could hear Roman and Andrea answering questions being put to them by Lieutenant Pirez. He continued to quiz them about what they knew of the perpetrator. Andrea couldn't tell them much as she'd never set eyes on the woman before and, of course, knew nothing of Miguel's previous marriage to Jennifer. Roman, on the other hand, was able to be more helpful, although he was never privy to what actually happened to Jennifer. He knew that Miguel's explanation of her mysterious disappearance was a fabric of lies. He ascribed that she had simply left him and he had tried to cover up the fact. Roman admitted that he and Miguel had previously been questioned by the police regarding the sudden disappearance of Gideon. Lieutenant Pirez informed Roman that Gideon's body had been found washed up on the shore with suspicious injures to his head. In fact, it had been concluded, after a post mortem by the forensic team, that he'd been struck over the head, from behind, with a wooden implement possibly an oar. Some wooden fragments had been found embedded in his skull, so he must have been hit with some force. However, this was not the cause of death, Gideon had drowned. Miguel and Roman had been economical with the truth as Miguel didn't want the police snooping into his affairs.

Roman was unable or unwilling to add anything more in his statement to Lieutenant Pirez, although the Lieutenant felt that Roman was concealing something. However there was no proof that Miguel and Roman were complicit in any way with Gideon's death. From what I could hear of the questions being fired at Roman it seemed the police had kept them under surveillance for some time. They suspected Miguel of being involved with drug trafficking but had no proof that would stand up in court and were unaware of Roman's involvement in the operation. When pushed by Lieutenant Pirez Roman admitted he had his suspicions about Miguel's activities but denied any involvement in criminality.

At worst he was guilty of not questioning where the money that supported their extravagant lifestyle had come from. He insisted that he was blissfully unaware of Miguel's drug deals. He had, he conceded, been naïve to say the least. Gideon, whose name derived from the Gideon Bible that was in the draw of the bedside cabinet of the grubby hotel where he was conceived had conspired with Miguel to keep the drug running side of their business away from Roman's gaze. From the snippets of conversation I could hear it seems that Gideon was more than a general dogsbody. He knew people! The right people! From the underworld and Miguel made full use of his expertise and contacts to expedite his criminal activities.

So now I knew the shocking truth about the man I'd married, although if he was still married to Jennifer our marriage would be null and void; however, that seemed pretty irrelevant now as I was going to die. Lieutenant Pirez sent two men down to put the corpses in their body bags. First they put Miguel in the bodybag closing the zip tight, then Jennifer's lifeless body was bagged up. Now finally my turn. I was beginning to feel some semblance of feeling returning to my battered body but I still couldn't communicate that I was still alive. Oh God I could feel the zip being pulled. What if they cremate me while I'm still alive! The thought terrified me. Miguel's body was first to be taken ashore, closely followed by Jennifer's. As they removed Jennifer's body the zip on her body bag had carelessly been partially unfastened and as her corpse was taken away her limp, lifeless hand flopped out of the bag revealing the diamond solitaire ring on her finger. Its former lustre diminished and stained with blood. I heard a gasp as Andrea watched, horrified, at the sight of Jennifer's corpse. Now it was my turn, the moment that the zip on the bodybag was closed. I feared I would not survive. As they were about to put me in the back of the van, next to the others, Lieutenant Pirez ordered them to stop.

"Wait, unzip that bag," Pirez ordered. "Something's bugging me; I don't know why but I just want to check that she's dead," Pirez explained to his stunned colleagues. As I felt the zip being slowly eased open I mustered all my strength and determination and managed to flicker my eyelids just as Pirez bent over the plastic body bag that threatened to entomb me. "She's alive, she's alive!" I could hear Pirez scream. "I think she winked at me. What's up with that incompetent fool of a doctor?" he shouted at the top of his voice. "Quick, get her into my jeep," he ordered. "There's no time to waste," he insisted. Thank God, I thought to myself. I knew my chances of survival were slim but at least then I had a chance. If it hadn't been for the diligence of Lieutenant Pirez and his premonition that made him look into the bag I would most certainly be leaving this mortal coil. As Pirez sped off sirens blaring he left the order that Silver Mist should be confiscated and held for further forensic examination. She was moved to a secluded bay to await removal, however, no guard had been posted to watch over her and in the late evening Silver Mist silently slipped her moorings and mysteriously sailed towards the horizon, her sails silhouetted against the darkening sky, navigated by her ghostly, crew never to be seen again.

Meanwhile Andrea and Roman were allowed to leave and they made their own way to the hospital Lieutenant Pirez was rushing me to. As we drove, at speed over the bumpy road, my mind was filled with guilt at the way I'd treated Andrea. Tricking Roman into having sex with me was wrong and I regretted it now; in fact, I regretted lots of things that I'd done. I promised God I would change and atone for my bad behaviour if only he'd let me live, like you do in times of crisis. It's funny how we all find religion when the chips are down but I genuinely knew that I would not be the same Susan if I were to survive. It seemed to take an age to get to the hospital, by now whatever drug I'd consumed was wearing off and I could feel and move slightly; however, that was a double-edged blade as I could now feel the full extent of my injuries. The pain was gruelling.

As we eventually arrived at the hospital and I was put on a trolley and wheeled hurriedly along a dimly lit corridor, I could hear the doctors saying, "It's touch and go, she's lost too much blood." At the end of the corridor double doors flung open and then nothing; I was slipping into a coma from which it would take me months to come out of. But when I did, who was there by my side, none other than Lieutenant Samuel Pirez with his rugged handsome features like the faces carved in Mount Rushmore. There was warmth and love in his eyes; he bent over my bed, a broad smile spreading across his face, his spirits uplifted by my re-emergence into the world of the living. As I panned my eyes around the private room in which I'd been cared for I was amazed to see so many flowers. It was like Kew Gardens! The smell of roses, gardenia, peonies and orchids filled the air with sweet aroma; the colours seemed so vibrant and their fragrance so intense.

Waking from a coma after six months all my senses were heightened to the point of exhilaration. I must have been close to death at one point. I could remember being drawn to a bright white light and I felt my body become weightless and floating towards that pure white light, but something pulled me back. Even during my darkest moments I could sense someone holding my hand. The nurses told me how Lieutenant Pirez had barely left my side; holding my hand and constantly talking to me, encouraging me to get well. This surely went beyond the call of duty.

"Hello," Lieutenant Pirez whispered as he held a glass of cold water to my parched lips. "Welcome back, Susan, it's been a long time," Pirez said.

I tried to speak but it was so difficult forming the words. I took another sip of water now, I began to whisper, "Who left all those flowers?" I tentatively enquired.

"Well some were from your friends, Roman and Andrea, and some from local well-wishers, and the rest from me," Lieutenant Pirez answered.

"Thank you," I said, tears welling up in my eyes. "Please thank everyone who's been caring for me; I feel so lucky to be alive," I went on. "I'm afraid Roman and Andrea left together to live in Italy, but they have kept in touch and have left contact details with me," Lieutenant

Pirez informed me. "I will let them know the good news as soon as I return to my office," Pirez went on. I was relieved that Roman and Andrea appeared to be making a go of it I would have hated the thought that I'd come between them, they were right for each other and Andrea deserved a bit of happiness.

Pirez and the nurse helped prop me up in bed and after a little more water I was able to talk a bit more. I wanted to quiz Pirez as to why he'd spent so much of his precious time by my side. "So have you been here all the time by my side?" I enquired.

"No, no," came his reply, "I just stopped by on the off chance; I pop in now and again to see how you are getting on and today I guess I got lucky."

"Okay," I quipped, "so why did the nurse say that you hardly left my side all these months?" Lieutenant Pirez looked away, embarrassed. He turned and looked at me sheepishly a nervous grin spread across his face. "Well maybe I did spend a lot more time by your side," Pirez admitted. "I was very concerned you were in such a bad way I was afraid you weren't going to make it," he went on. "To be honest, Susan, since that day when you managed to flutter your eyes at me to confirm that you were still alive I've been captivated by you and I've rehearsed in my mind what I would say to you when you woke up, but now you have, I don't know what to say." Pirez spilled out his heart.

I mustered up my strength and reached for his hand and clasped it tightly in my own. "Can I call you Samuel? I believe that is what the nurses called you," I enquired. "Lieutenant Pirez seems a bit formal, don't you think?"

Samuel nodded in agreement. "Samuel, my love, you saved my life, if it wasn't for you I'd be dead, no question about it," I said re-assuredly. I looked into his eyes and instantly felt a connection; it wouldn't be long before I was totally under his spell.

The next few months of rehabilitation weren't easy but with Samuel by my side, encouraging and cajoling me, it wasn't long before I could dispense with the crutches and walk unaided around the beautiful hospital gardens, albeit very gingerly. Samuel and I became closer and romance between us blossomed. Samuel was divorced and lived a lonely bachelor existence, the demands of his job taking their toll on his marriage. Being married to a committed policeman like Samuel would take a special type of woman. Was I that type of woman? I wondered. Looking deep into my heart I knew I was and if he asked me to marry him I'll accept without hesitation. I know my track record of choosing men wasn't that good but I decided that I wouldn't let my horrific experience with Miguel put me off men forever. I instinctively knew that Samuel was the man for me and as I previously stated I am not the same Susan that came to the Caribbean for adventure all those months ago. Soon I was well enough to leave hospital and Samuel asked me to move in with him, an invitation l gladly accepted.

On our first evening together I made him a nice meal and I lit some candles and poured the chilled wine. I did my best to promote a feeling of romance. I am not the best cook in the world but it was a magnitude better than the take-away meals that Samuel was used to. After finishing our meal we went up to the bedroom to consummate our love for one another. I think we were both nervous. I was worried that my experiences would make me frigid and didn't want to let him down. I still had some nasty scars on my torso. I knew Samuel had seen them but still I felt uncomfortable. On his part, he was scared of physically hurting me. Fortunately all these worries were quickly dismissed as we made love in sublime ecstasy. He was so gentle and caring and did all he could to excite and please me. This is what it was like to make love as opposed to having sex. A warm feeling of satisfaction came over me as Samuel finally came inside of me, filling me with a sensuous glow that I'm sure showed in my flushed cheeks.

All was sheer bliss for months until, one day, Samuel informed me that his mother had an affair and that he was the result of her infidelity. His biological father was English, though he knew precious little about him. His mother was unable to tell him much as the affair was short-lived, his only reference was a black and white photograph taken while he'd stayed on the island. It seemed his mother had the affair because his father, himself a police officer, put his career before their relationship. She'd felt neglected and increasingly frustrated at her husband's lack of interest in her. Samuel admitted to me that his first marriage had ended in similar circumstances, but he'd learnt his lesson and was determined not to let his work ruin any future relationship. "I think you know how much I love you, Susan," Samuel said, looking dreamingly into my eyes. "I want you to be my wife, but before you give me your answer I wanted you to know all there is to know about me, I don't want any secrets between us," Samuel explained. He held out his hand holding the photo of his biological father. "This is the man I told you about, I've never tried to find him and probably never will but I just want to share whatever baggage I'm carrying with you," Samuel said. I took the photo and glanced at it casually, my heart started pounding and my eyes nearly shot out of their sockets. I couldn't believe it. Shit! I recognised the man in the photo immediately, it was Uncle Eric. Oh bollocks that would make us cousins wouldn't it? And worse I've screwed Samuel's father.

How could I ever begin to tell him that Eric was my uncle and, by the way, I fucked him several times. What would that say about me, what would he think of me then? No! I think I'd better keep this bombshell to myself, I thought, and hope he's never tempted to find his biological father. Just one more misdemeanour for my conscious to deal with, especially after what Samuel had said about not having any secrets from each other. I couldn't believe my past indiscretions could come back to haunt me so cruelly. All Samuel knew about Eric was that he lived in a small village in Oxford, England, but if he was inclined to look for him it wouldn't take too much research, especially for a detective. Uncle Eric had told me numerous stories about his travels in the Caribbean but never mentioned anything about an affair, the randy bastard. No wonder my longsuffering aunt had left him long ago. On reflection, I asked myself the question again. Should I own up and tell the truth, or keep quiet. A quandary indeed! I looked wistfully into Samuel's mournful eyes, "If that was your idea of a proposal, Samuel," I said ruefully, "Of course I'll marry you. I'd be proud to be your wife," I said flinging my arms around his neck. "You know, my darling, you shouldn't spend too much time thinking about your biological father, I'm sure he's never given you a moment's thought," I said. "I'm sure to him it was just a bit of fun he would have forgotten about as soon as he'd packed his bags for Blighty. No, it's the man who brought you up and provided for you all those years and accepted you as his son that's most important and you should never lose sight of that," I advised lovingly. Of course, I had my own ulterior motive for dissuading him from searching for his birth father. Well, what would you do?

16

Time to meet Samuel's mum and dad. Although they were divorced they still had an amicable relationship which would make things much easier for me. I won't feel pressured into taking sides or blaming anyone for the breakup of their marriage. I wanted to be accepted and befriend them both, if possible. Of course, I wanted them to like me and hoped they would welcome Samuel and my union, but I was nervous about what questions they might bombard me with. Clearly Samuel had pre-warned them of the circumstances of our meeting and they were acutely aware of my fragility. Things were still pretty raw in my mind. It's impossible to dismiss something as traumatic as to what I had witnessed and gone through, no matter how determined I was to live a normal happy life. I needn't have worried about how I would be received, they were truly lovely towards me and seemed genuinely happy for us both. I must say I was relieved to come away with the feeling of acceptance and a feeling to real warmth towards me.

Over the coming weeks I was paraded around the rest of Samuel's family and all seemed happy to accept me into the family. Samuel had a sister that he'd spoken little of, he felt that she somehow blamed him for their parents splitting up. I soon struck up a friendship with her, she and I clicked from the start. Maybe if Zena and I could forge a strong friendship it would help repair her and Samuel's relationship. Whatever, I would do my best to foster good relations between us. Not having had a brother or sister myself I think it sad for siblings to be estranged. Anyway, from a selfish point of view, I needed someone to help me organise by big day. With Andrea so far away I needed a friend to help me choose my wedding dress and accessories and, with Zena's local knowledge, a fitting venue for our nuptials. I for one favoured a simple plain affair with not too much fuss. I think Samuel was of similar mind; after all, it was his second marriage and all the pomp and ceremony of the first certainly didn't spell a recipe for success. Nor indeed, had my non marriage to Miguel been a success, so under the circumstances it suited both of us to keep it simple.

When Samuel and I went to the jewellers to choose our wedding rings it suddenly occurred to me that I would have to wear my ring on my right hand because I lost my wedding ring finger during Jennifer's onslaught. It was only now that Samuel chose to tell me of all the facts relating to my ordeal. For the first time I had some sympathy with Jennifer and although she nearly killed me, perhaps, what she did saved me from an even worse fate. After what Jennifer had been through it was no wonder she was mentally unbalanced. Maybe now I know what had driven the poor wretch to act as she did I could allow the healing process to get under way and put the whole experience behind me once and for all. My physical scars had healed, it was the psychological ones that remained.

I excitedly wrote to Andrea to tell her the news and to invite her and Roman to my forthcoming wedding, knowing that they had themselves married whilst I was still in my coma, which, although I was happy for them I missed the chance to be a bridesmaid. Like most girls I dreamt one day I would be a bridesmaid. I would now offer that privilege to Andrea, and of course to Zena. Andrea, now being married, would be my Maid of Honour. A week after writing to Andrea I received a reply. She was she said absolutely thrilled for me, but she had some news for me too. She informed me gleefully that she was expecting a baby. Our reunion would be a special moment with much to celebrate. I also mentioned by predicament about Uncle Eric and pleaded with her not to allude to him in any way, and if by any chance Samuel were to show her his photo would she please not show any sign that she'd seen him before. Andrea was quite happy to go along with my deception as she didn't want Roman to know about her liaisons with Uncle Eric. When I told Samuel that I'd written to Andrea inviting her and Roman to the wedding he looked at me with a worried frown.

"Of course I expected you to invite them, Susan," Samuel said with resignation in his voice, "but you'd better warn them to be very careful when they return to Haiti."

"Why?" I asked. "Is there something you haven't told me?"

"Well while you were in the coma and before they

left the island, they confided in me about what they'd witnessed in the jungle." Samuel explained. "They'd seen a young girl raped and murdered in a voodoo satanic ceremony," he went on. "I tried to investigate their claims but was prevented from looking too deeply into the alleged incident," Samuel carried on. "Someone in high office had blocked my enquiries and the message was that if I wanted to keep my rank I'd better drop it." "I know the tentacles of the Satanist hierarchy stretched far and wide, there are people in my own station I don't trust." Samuel carried on, "If these people think Roman and Andrea could threaten them in any way their lives could be in danger," Samuel cautioned. "I'll have to keep a close eye on them when they return," Samuel exclaimed. The horror on my face obviously showed. "Don't worry, Susan, I promise I'll keep them safe but it would be just as well that they don't stay too long after the wedding," Samuel said, with some degree of trepidation in his voice.

17

It's the day of my wedding and everything's going to plan and my hair is being styled by a friend of Samuel's sister. Zena has been a real godsend helping me choose my dress and the venue, relieving me of a lot of the logistics. In the absence of my best friend Andrea, Zena has been a rock. Samuel has picked up Roman and Andrea from the airport and as promised he has not let them out of his sight. I can't wait to see Andrea again, I've missed her more than I realised! We would have so much to talk about and to celebrate, with the wonderful news of her pregnancy. It also occurred to me that Samuel and I hadn't discussed having children. I don't know if he expects us to start a family; it's not something I have thought about before now. I must admit I've never been that maternal but I wasn't dead against the idea of motherhood, it's just that I've never thought about it. I now realise how rushed everything has been. Still there were no doubts in my mind at all about marrying Samuel. He is a wonderful man and I think I've been quite lucky, in retrospect, to have found him. Just as I finish varnishing my nails the door opens and in walks Andrea with Roman by her side, a suitcase in each hand. Samuel has dropped them off and was on his way back to his best friend's house to get ready for the wedding. Ambrose, his best friend from school, was to be his best man.

We have a spare room and insisted that Roman and Andrea stayed with us for the week, that way Samuel could keep an eye on them, without alarming them in any way. Samuel and I weren't planning to go away on honeymoon till some time later when he could arrange cover for himself at work. "Put those cases down and go and pour yourselves a drink, Roman," I invited. "Come here, Andrea, give me a hug I've missed you so much," I said, tears welling up in my eyes. "You look amazing, darling, being pregnant obviously suits you, you look positively radiant I've never see quite so much colour in your cheeks before," I said.

"Hello Susan," Andrea replied "I've missed you too," her eyes filled with tears as she hugged me. "How have you been?" Andrea enquired, "You look so well and, to be honest, the last time I saw you," Andrea paused for a moment, holding back the emotion, "I thought you wouldn't make it." She went on as she recovered her composure. "And look at you now about to become Mrs Pirez. Roman and I are so happy for you," Andrea's voice quivering with emotion.

Looking down at Andrea's bump I wondered if I'd made enough allowance in her bridesmaid's dress to disguise her condition, not that I am sure she would want to hide it, but to make her feel more comfortable, especially in the midday heat. Andrea took my hand and led me into a quiet corner but by now the house was full of family members, friends, hair stylist, and make-up specialist, etc. "I need to tell you something Susan." Andrea looked quite serious for a moment as she had some bad news for me. Well, I don't know if I would call it bad under the circumstances. I was used to bad news and nothing shocked me these days. She went on to explain that she"d heard through a mutal friend that my Uncle Eric had sadly passed away. Oh my God, I thought to myself, putting my hand over my mouth. I enquired as to how he'd met his fate.

"Well, you're not going to believe this, or perhaps you will." Andrea, smiling ruefully, informed me that he'd had a heart attack whilst humping a woman half his age. I was stunned for moment. It took a while for the irony to sink in and the sudden realisation that I was off the hook.

"Oh that's terrible," I said trying not to giggle. We looked at each other and burst into fits of laughter. I know it seems rather disrespectful, laughing at his demise, but it's the way he would have wanted to go, the horny old git. I wondered how many other illegitimate children he had fathered with his wandering dick. Today would be even better than I had hoped, this news lifted a weight off my shoulders, perhaps now I could put the past firmly behind me.

Soon I was standing at the altar next to Samuel hearing those immortal words, "Now I pronounce you man and wife, you may kiss the bride." Samuel kissed me, his lips lingering on mine as he stared lovingly into my eyes. This will be a new chapter in my life, I thought, and I'm not going to mess it up. Zena and Andrea looked gorgeous in their dresses and Andrea's dress fitted like a dream in the end. The festivities were well under way and the drink flowed freely, not that I drank much myself and Andrea, being pregnant, couldn't drink either. The boys, of course, had their fill as did my new sister-in-law, Zena. Still she deserved to have a good time for all the help she had afforded me. The best man's speech passed as best man's speeches normally do, leaving Samuel red-faced. He'd been quite a lad in his yesteryears it transpired. Samuel's mum and dad made a good fist of getting on during the course of the evening, easing any tension that might have spoilt the day.

Samuel and I left early, thanking and hugging our guests as we departed. With Roman and Andrea staying with us, we knew we wouldn't have much privacy. Samuel and I were so comfortable with each other that we didn't feel the need to make love on our wedding night, we just cuddled up in bed, knowing we had the rest of our lives together. Andrea and Roman arrived home in the early hours. I heard the key in the door and Andrea giggle as Roman tripped up the step, apparently worse for wear, then the bedroom door closing and remembered no more until the morning. The sun was streaming through the blinds, we must have overslept. "Shit, it's ten o'clock!" I shouted in Samuel's ear, not considering he might be hungover.

"Okay," Samuel responded, "It's not a problem, is it? We've got nothing special to get up for."

"We've got guests don't forget," I reminded him. "Okay, yes, you're right I'll just have a shower and I'll be down," Samuel insisted.

I put on one of my more decent dressing gowns and

went downstairs. Roman and Andrea were already up and had prepared a sumptuous breakfast for Samuel and me.

"Good morning. Good night, was it?" Andrea winked at me.

"Oh, you know so so," I replied. "Good morning, Roman, how's your head this morning?" I asked. "Good morning, Susan," Roman responded. "Could you speak softly," he pleaded. Well that answered that question, I thought to myself. Shortly Samuel came down and we all ate the hearty breakfast, even those with sore heads. Samuel's sister had, by all accounts, been very drunk but had made it home safely. I bet she's suffering this morning, I pondered.

After a week of reliving happy memories it was time for Andrea and Roman to leave and head back home to Italy. There were hugs and tears as I waved goodbye to my old friend, emotion flooding through my veins. I wished her well and hoped all would go smoothly during the birth of her baby. I begged her to let me know as soon as the child was born. As I watched the plane climb into the air a feeling of sadness and loss came over me. Samuel gently took my hand and led me away; he understood the strength of the bond between us. I comforted myself with the thought that I had a wonderful life ahead of me with a man I loved and cherished.

Four months passed when I received a letter from Andrea informing me that she'd had her baby, a gorgeous little boy they'd called Romares. He weighed a staggering ten pounds and the poor girl had a difficult delivery, but all was well now. I wrote back to say I was delighted by her news and sent my love and congratulations along with a small gift for the newborn. As the years passed Andrea and I kept in constant touch, even visiting one another on occasions. Soon Romares had started school and was sent the latest photos and even a clipping of his hair. I felt like a real auntie to Romares as he grew up to be a well behaved and well adjusted teenager.

Samuel and I have a loving marriage and a good social life, however as much as I've tried, it's been impossible for me to forget that fateful night Jennifer tried to kill me. I wake up at night in a cold sweat, reliving that awful moment. I've had therapy but every time we go anywhere near the part of the island where I was left for dead, memories come back to haunt me. For this reason Samuel decided to apply for a new position in the St. Martin Police Force with the view to both of us moving there. He was successful with his application and even managed to get promotion. Once we'd sold up and moved to St. Martin I felt a huge weight lifted off of me, as if being reborn, I felt rejuvenated and full of life again. Samuel had grown tired of constantly looking over his shoulder on Haiti because he didn't trust his superiors and always felt that he was being watched. He knew there were many corrupt officers around him and they knew he knew, which put him in constant danger, so Samuel was as relieved as I was to start a new life on St. Martin. St. Martin was always my favourite of all the islands we visited.

I let Andrea and Roman know we had moved and gave her our current address. Andrea wrote to say how pleased she was that we'd moved from Haiti; she too hated returning there whenever they visited and she felt sure that I would be much happier now free from the voodoo spell that seemed to paralyse me. Andrea had some news to share with me too: Romares was going to study at a top university in England. She knew she would miss his sunny effervescent disposition.

Everyday life goes on at such a pace that it's hard to see where all the years have gone. I'm now happier than I've ever been in my life and for someone who was not a bit maternal, I now have two beautiful children. Martin, named after our new home, and Katrina, after that infamous storm. I've just had some slightly disturbing news from Andrea: on the plus side she informs me with considerable pride that Romares has graduated with a degree, a 2.1 no less in his chosen field. On the negative side Romares had met and fell in love with a lovely young English girl who was very upper class and spoke in a soft aristocratic voice. She walked out of a theological lecture and into Romares's life. Once they'd met she only had eyes for him and he'd never seen her before around the campus, it was if she suddenly appeared out of nowhere, like an angel sent from heaven to be by his side.

The first time he looked into her steely eyes it was like an interstellar burst of light. She just appeared like a spectre out of the mists of time, like a goddess propelled through time and space to land at his adoring feet. They got on so well together and they had the same interests and the same appetite for rumbustious sex. She seemed so experienced and taught young Romares how to pleasure a woman. Even though Romares had never met her before he had a strange feeling of déjà vu. After

Romares had finished his course he returned home with his new love to introduce her to Roman and Andrea.

The moment Andrea opened the door to Romares her heart froze. "Hello Mum," Romares said. "This is my fiancé, Jennifer." Jennifer held out her hand to shake Andrea's. It was ice cold! "Hello Andrea, Romares has told me so much about you. I'm sorry, you look startled," Jennifer went on.

"Oh I'm sorry it's just a bit of a shock, that's all," Andrea replied. "You send your son off to university as a boy and he comes back a man engaged," Andrea continued. Roman held out his hand to welcome Jennifer into their home.

"That's a very expensive-looking engagement ring," Roman suggested. "Perhaps I should reduce your allowance, Romares," he said jokingly.

"Oh," Romares laughed, "I didn't buy the ring; it's far grander than anything I could afford. It's a ring that Jennifer was given by her former love, who unfortunately, died suddenly." Romares added, "I'm happy for her to wear the ring, at least until I can buy her one myself, but that might be sometime hence," Romares explained. The ring had a strange pattern with flecks of red embedded in the brilliant white diamond, almost like splatters of blood.

"We have some news that we want you to know first," Romares said. "Jennifer is going to have my baby," Andrea and Roman gasped in unison. "I'm sorry to spring this on you but I think it's important that you both know," Romares concluded. Roman and Andrea regained their composure. "Come here. Congratulations, give your mum a hug," requested Andrea. "Yes, congratulations both of you," Roman said reluctantly, still in a state of shock.

"Jennifer's had a scan and we're having a little boy," Romares explained. "We're going to call him Miguel after someone Jennifer once knew long ago," he added. A hushed silence ensued. Andrea's sense of foreboding was palpable, even from several thousand miles away. Roman and Andrea looked into Jennifer's cool steely gaze and then looked at each other with the haunting question on their lips: would they ever be free from the pull of the voodoo curse that has blighted their lives since that ill-fated Caribbean adventure?

I felt my heart racing and pulse quicken at this unwelcome news. It made me wonder if I was really free of the influences of the voodoo curse that threatened to engulf us all.